A MATCH MADE
in Duty

To all who sacrifice to keep us safe

CHAPTER 1

London, England
October 1815

JAMES BRAYDEN, FIFTH Earl of Exmoor, glanced at the bottle of brandy his butler had just carried in on a sparkling silver tray and set down beside him on the elegant mahogany desk in his study. He waited for his butler to depart and close the door behind him before turning to the two guests who had just arrived and were about to change his life forever. "Care for a drink, Major Allworthy?"

Ordinarily, he would have given his friend, Lawrence Allworthy, an amiable pat on the back and poured them both a tall glass of the fiery amber liquid his butler had just brought in. Ordinarily, they would have settled in the cushioned leather chairs beside the blazing fire and spent the night getting drunk while reminiscing about the men in their regiment and the years spent on the Continent battling Napoleon's forces. Ordinarily, their first order of business would have been to toast their fallen companions.

But tonight was no ordinary night. His gaze settled on the young woman with lustrous dark hair and big, brown eyes who stood quietly beside his friend. "And you, Miss Wilkinson. May I offer you tea? Refreshments? The journey could not have been an easy one for you."

"No, thank you." She blushed as she spoke and then looked down at her toes, obviously wishing to be anywhere but in his study.

James decided the rose blush was quite becoming on her cheeks.

He leaned on his cane to slowly walk around the sturdy desk that dominated the center of the room and came to stand beside his guests. Up close, he could see that the young woman was trembling, though she did

2 | MEARA PLATT

her best to hide her fear as he approached. Were his scars so hideous? He supposed they were, for even he had yet to grow used to them. They'd be most alarming to a stranger. "Please," James said, motioning to the chairs beside the fireplace. "This will be your home soon, Miss Wilkinson. You may as well get used to it."

She pinched her lips and frowned lightly. "I don't wish to be rude, Lord Exmoor. But what makes you think I wish to accept your proposal?"

He exchanged glances with Lawrence who appeared as surprised by her remark as he was. "It was your brother's dying request that I marry you. I promised him that I would and I intend to honor that vow."

Her pink blush deepened. "Do I have no say in the matter?" She tipped her chin up to meet his gaze, and although she was small and slender, the top of her head barely reaching his shoulder, he could see that she had a full-sized, stubborn determination.

Lawrence cleared his throat. "Miss Wilkinson, what choice do you have? Do you not wish to marry an earl? I do not know of any young woman in your circumstances who would refuse–"

"Major Allworthy," James said, quietly interrupting him. "I think it is best that I speak on my behalf." He understood the young lady's reluctance now that she'd taken a good look at him, and expected that she was now quietly swallowing her revulsion. While his leg would hopefully strengthen in time, the jagged scars etched on his face were permanent and unfortunately, too prominent to hide. "No doubt the terms of our arrangement must concern you. We ought to go over them now, for you may have some misconceptions about what... ah, I shall expect in your duties as my wife."

He raked a hand through his hair. "Perhaps we ought to speak about this matter in private. Major Allworthy... Lawrence, would you mind giving us a moment alone?"

His friend appeared to be as uncomfortable as James was and more than eager to leave this embarrassing discussion to him. "Excellent idea. I'll be in your library. I'm sure there's a book I'm eager to read." He dashed out as though his coattails were on fire.

The girl appeared desperate to follow him out, but James placed a light hand on her elbow to hold her back. "Give me a moment of your time, Miss Wilkinson. Hear me out before you walk out of here." He cast her a wry smile. "Or run out. I wouldn't blame you."

She relented with a curt nod.

"Please, let's sit beside the warming fire." He settled her in one of the chairs and took the other. She must have noticed the awkward way he sank into the soft maroon leather and stretched his leg in front of him since he could not yet bend it. But she said nothing, and to her credit, made no moue of distaste.

"I know this isn't easy for you," he said, uncertain how one politely raised the issue of the bedchamber to a young woman one had known for all of two minutes. Yet, that particularly thorny issue had to be foremost on her mind and James knew he had to address it immediately. "Rest assured that I will not... er..." *Bloody humiliating!* In all his days, he never imagined himself in this awkward situation. Before the war, he had been considered quite the catch. Beautiful young women threw themselves in his path with tedious regularity, all of them eager to gain his notice in the hope they might become the next Countess Exmoor.

Now, they darted away in the hope of avoiding him. All but the most desperate and browbeaten debutantes whose families were in dire need of funds to maintain their estates. He ran a hand across the back of his neck in consternation. "I promised your brother I would take care of you. He extracted my promise to marry you, for he feared your cousin would not be generous with you once he took title to your brother's holdings. His fears obviously proved correct. What would you have done had Major Allworthy and his wife not been at hand to bring you to London?"

Her face began to heat and he knew it had nothing to do with the heat of the flames burning in the hearth. "I would have managed, my lord. I am not your charity case."

"Indeed, you are not."

"My lord," she said more insistently as she met his gaze. "I agreed to accompany Major Allworthy in the hope that you might help me find suitable employment."

He arched an eyebrow. "You're asking me to renege on my promise to your brother?" In truth, he liked that directness about her and the fact that she did not flinch when looking at him. "I cannot do it, Miss Wilkinson. I'm offering to make you my wife. In truth, I'd be honored if you accepted. I know I'm rather a poor specimen."

She quirked a soft eyebrow in what appeared to be surprise. Was she disputing the obvious? "Certainly not the husband you might have hoped for," he continued, "but you will always be safe here and treated with honor." He cleared his throat. "You shall have your own bedchamber, of course. And I shall not impose on you."

Lord! How much plainer could he state that he'd keep his hands off her?

Her only response was a slight widening of her big, chocolate brown eyes, so he continued the uncomfortable conversation. "I am under no illusions. The war took its toll on all of us. Whatever hopes or dreams I may have had…" He motioned toward his face. "Well, I'm no longer any woman's idea of perfection."

Her lips turned upward in the hint of a smile. "My lord, may I be impertinent?"

He much preferred it to her being a timid mouse around him. "Of course."

"You seem to think I'm a simple-brained ninny and that my only requirement in a husband is a man with a pretty face. I assure you, I am not that shallow." She let out a soft sigh and leaned closer so that he caught the subtle scent of lavender soap along her slender throat. "I will not deny that my situation is dire. But that does not give me the right to interfere with your future happiness. As you can see, I have little polish. I'm no society gem." She shook her head and sighed again. "How can you possibly think to make me your countess? I'm a penniless stranger with no family connections."

"I gave your brother my word and I intend to keep it. I would do the same if you had the face of a wart hog or the brain of a goose. Thankfully, you have neither of those qualities. All I ask is that you live under my roof – separate quarters, of course – and act as my hostess when the need arises for me to entertain at home. I would also ask that you accompany me to the balls and other social engagements to which we shall be invited."

She tipped her head and nibbled her lip as she studied him, her gaze once again direct and assessing. "A business arrangement."

"Yes." He nodded. "You shall have an allowance, of course. Your days will be mostly your own."

"I see." She stood and had the courtesy to pretend to study the flames brightly glowing in the hearth while he struggled to his feet in order to stand beside her. "I suppose we ought to shake hands to seal our bargain."

Was she accepting his terms?

She stuck out her small, gloved hand to confirm it.

He wasn't used to shaking hands with a woman, for those of his acquaintance merely dangled their fingers before him in expectation that he would bow over them and mutter some polite inanity. But Miss Wilkinson, although quite genteel in her looks and manners, had a no nonsense way about her. He set his cane aside and swallowed her hand in both of his. "Done."

He expected a trumpet fanfare. A chorus of angels singing. A tremor along the ground, for the prospect of marriage was no small matter. But all was silent. Even Miss Wilkinson was holding her breath, no doubt contemplating the bargain she'd just made. "One small request," he said, still holding her hand and noting that she'd made no move to slip it out of his grasp. "In public, I shall call you Lady Exmoor. But I'd hoped for something less formal when we are alone at home. What is your given name?"

She laughed lightly and shook her head. "Did my brother neglect to mention it?"

James cast her a wincing smile. "He mentioned it a time or two, but more often he referred to you as... Smidge."

She couldn't help but laugh again, but that melodic trill was punctuated with a groan. "Oh, dear! That was the awful pet name he gave me when we were children. I hope you will banish it from your memory at once! My name is Sophie."

"Sophie," he repeated softly. "Nice to meet you. I'm James."

CHAPTER 2

"NICE TO MEET you, my lord." Sophie placed a hand over her quickening heart to still its rapid beat. Lord Exmoor had taken hold of her other hand to seal their bargain and she was surprised by how nice his touch felt. His palms were rough and calloused, she could tell even through the soft fabric of her glove. But there was a gentleness in the way he held her hand that could not be denied.

"Oh, that won't do." He shook his head and regarded her with such seriousness, that she thought he was going to berate her. Just what she had done to overset him was a mystery. In the next moment, his expression lightened. "My name is James, as I've just told you. Obviously, you must address me as Exmoor or my lord when in the presence of others."

She nodded.

"But I hope you will call me James whenever we are alone. Such as now." He tipped his head toward her and for a mad instant, she thought he might kiss her. For an even madder, fleeting moment, she thought she might just want to kiss him back.

No, she was merely caught up in the surprising bargain they had just struck. She was about to go from being destitute to becoming the next Countess Exmoor. What's more, the man she would soon marry appeared to have many of the qualities she'd hoped for in a husband. Kindness, honor, and he was physically appealing as well. He was big and muscled, and if one looked past the scars on his face, one saw the fine cut of his jaw and the intelligence behind his dark emerald eyes. He had a full head of blond hair, a dark, golden blond like the gold of the sun as it rose over the moors at daybreak. "James," she said in a whisper.

Major Allworthy coughed once to gain their attention. She hadn't realized he had returned and was standing behind her.

"Ah, Lawrence." Lord Exmoor glanced over her shoulder to

acknowledge his companion and at the same time released her hand. "Seems we are in business."

The major smiled as he addressed her. "Lord Exmoor will obtain the special license tomorrow and you shall be married the day after that. Do you have any objections to the arrangement, Miss Wilkinson?"

"No. Now that we are in agreement, there is no need to delay the inevitable." In truth, she was relieved and quite grateful for the rescue. She had no idea where else she could have gone now that her ungracious cousin had tossed her out of the only home she'd ever known. Fortunately, Major Allworthy and his wife, who also resided in York, had taken her in immediately.

She and Lady Allworthy had become good friends over the years and would often meet to share correspondence from Sophie's brother or the major since the men were in the same regiment and often had news to relate about each other. The two men had formed a strong bond of friendship in the heat of battle. Their third brother-in-arms was Lord Exmoor. In truth, Sophie felt as though she already knew this man who would soon become her husband because her brother so often mentioned him in his letters.

But it was only after Harry had died, a mere month ago, that she'd learned of the promise Lord Exmoor had made to him. By the somber looks the major and his wife had cast each other on the ride down from York to London, she'd expected to meet an ogre.

Lord Exmoor was anything but that.

In truth, she thought him ruggedly handsome.

However, she hesitated to mention it since even he was under the impression that he was hideous to women. Had she attempted to assure him that he was not, she doubted he would have believed her. Likely, he would have put her squarely in the category of women who would sacrifice their bodies to gain his wealth and title.

She wasn't that at all.

If he changed his mind and wanted out of the bargain they'd just made, she would agree. After all, he was the one being burdened with a wife not of his choosing. In exchange, she might impose upon him to find her employment in a respectable household, perhaps as companion to an elderly dowager, but that would be the extent of her demands. More of a request, really. She had no intention of holding him up if he wished to back out of the wedding.

Sophie remained silent as she and Major Allworthy left Lord Exmoor's fashionable townhouse in Belgravia and returned by carriage to the equally fashionable Allworthy residence on Chipping Way in Mayfair. The residence belonged to his somewhat eccentric grandfather, General Allworthy, and Sophie had immediately taken a liking to the old man. Although gruff on the outside, he had a kind heart and had made her feel welcome the moment she'd entered his home a mere two days ago.

Both houses were far more beautiful than any she'd ever resided in.

"My wife and I do not maintain our own residence in London," the major explained on the short ride back to Chipping Way. "We prefer to stay with my grandfather. He grumbles and blusters but looks forward to our visits and is quite sad when we leave. Lady Allworthy and I would love to have him reside with us in York, but he won't hear of it. I'll worry about the old badger when we return north."

Sophie was grateful to the major and his wife for all they'd done for her, so she was eager to repay their kindness in some small way. "If Lord Exmoor permits it, I would be happy to visit your grandfather from time to time. Indeed, it seems the perfect solution since I will be living nearby. I could visit him at least once a week when I'm... oh, dear. Oh, dear. It feels quite strange to think of myself as Lady Exmoor."

The major misunderstood her concern and leaned forward to pat her hand. "Be patient with Exmoor. He may have lost his good looks, but he has a good and noble heart."

She merely nodded. What was wrong with everyone? She had two functioning eyes. Yes, he had scars. Long, hideous ones to be sure. But they did not detract from his fine features.

The rest of the day passed quickly. Sophie and the major's wife, Lydia, spent the afternoon shopping for elegant shoes and a delicate, apricot silk fabric to make a new gown. After all, she couldn't marry an earl in a serviceable wool gown and brown boots. Lydia refused to hear any protest about the cost. "Consider this as our wedding gift to you."

Sophie began working on the gown as soon as they returned to the townhouse. She retired to her quarters and sewed for several hours until suppertime. That evening, she and the Allworthys were invited to their neighbors, the Farthingales, who were having a dinner party. John and Sophie Farthingale – they'd shared a laugh over their shared name – seemed to understand her trepidation over her upcoming nuptials. "There will be gossip about your wedding," Sophie Farthingale said with a doleful shake of her head, "but it will be tame compared to the misadventures my daughters managed to find themselves in." She glanced down the table at her two youngest who were identical twins. "I shudder to think what chaos they'll create when it's their turn."

Sophie followed her gaze. "Your daughters, Lily and Daffodil? But they look so sweet." The girls had dark hair and big, blue eyes, and the only way to tell them apart was that Lily wore spectacles that kept sliding down her pert nose.

"Looks are deceiving," their mother said with a wistful smile. "But as for you, Sophie, keep strong. I know Exmoor has had a bad time of it, what with his injuries. Sometimes the scars run quite deep. All the more reason he needs a good woman to love. The gossip will stop once you settle into your marriage. Do stop by whenever you feel the need to talk."

"I will. Thank you, Mrs. Farthingale." She didn't bother to reveal that their marriage was a sham, a business arrangement and nothing more. She expected everyone seated at the table knew it already, for earls did not fall in love at first sight with ordinary young women or offer to marry them in the very next moment.

Although the eventful day had exhausted her, Sophie spent a restless night and awoke dreading what this new dawn would bring. She was certain Lord Exmoor's proposal had only been a dream and she was about to discover her true fate. She washed and dressed, and forced a smile on her face so that her disposition appeared as bright and sunny as this crisp, October day.

She loved the slight chill to the air and the incredible blue of the sky. She loved the reds and golds of the changing leaves on the trees at this time of the year.

Autumn colors suited her complexion best, however she'd chosen the apricot silk for her bridal gown because it was a soft color of spring, and spring was a time of new lambs and calves and foals coming into the world, a time for new beginnings.

A time for hope.

By noon she, Lydia, and the major were on their way to Lord Exmoor's home in order to make final arrangements for the wedding. Lord Exmoor greeted them politely and escorted them into his dining room for a light repast of cold ham that had been cooked in a honey glaze and duck in a chestnut puree that was the tastiest thing Sophie had eaten in ages.

She felt Lord Exmoor's gaze on her much of the time and wondered if her table manners were up to his standard. Although they maintained an easy banter, she couldn't help but think that any moment now, he was going to beg out of their agreement. "Shall we retire to my study?" he suggested as they finished their meal.

Much as Sophie had enjoyed the repast, she'd eaten very little. And spoke very little after they entered the study. Major Allworthy and his wife settled on the sofa while she and Lord Exmoor took chairs opposite them. A cozy fire burned in the hearth and the butler wheeled in tea and cakes to munch on while they made their wedding plans.

Good heavens!

By tomorrow, she'd be married.

As the discussion of their wedding progressed, Sophie began to fidget and shift uncomfortably. "I thought it was to be a simple ceremony, just the major and his wife as witnesses. Are we to have many guests?"

Lord Exmoor grimaced. "No, but I have family in town that I must invite. My sister and her husband, and my younger brother. My aunts and a few cousins." Suddenly, he paused and shook his head. "Blast, but I'm dense. Forgive my thoughtlessness. Is there anyone you wish to invite?"

He appeared sincerely distressed by the oversight, so she hastened to assure him that with her brother now gone, there was no one in all of England she would care to ask. "I look forward to meeting your family. I hope they are as nice as you."

His dark emerald eyes widened in surprise. "You think I'm nice?"

Her smiled slipped as she studied his darkening expression. "Aren't you?" Major Allworthy had spoken so highly of him, as had her brother in his letters to her. She never considered that he was not. "That is…" She gripped the arm of her chair and turned her pleading gaze to Lydia Allworthy.

The lovely woman was perhaps in her late twenties, only about eight years older than Sophie, but she had far more experience dealing with men and seemed to understand her concerns at once. "He and my husband may toss back brandies together a little too often for my liking, but they rarely allow their drinking to get out of hand. Indeed, I've never seen Lord Exmoor imbibe too much. Or behave irresponsibly or impolitely. If anything, he is too much in control. I think that is Lord Exmoor's only fault. In all other aspects, he is a man of intelligence and honor. In other words, no. He doesn't gamble and he won't beat you when he's drunk."

"Lydia!" Major Allworthy began to sputter in horror.

Lord Exmoor frowned. "Miss Wilkinson, I may look like a repulsive beast, but I've never raised a hand to a woman and never will."

"Repulsive?" Sophie curled her hands into fists and shot to her feet, now decidedly angry with him and with everyone else who made him feel lesser. "If you dare call yourself that again, my lord, it is I who shall take my fists to you. And you had better not even *think* that way about yourself. My cousin is repulsive. You are noble and heroic."

His eyebrow shot up and a wry grin crossed his lips. "Do you hear that Lawrence? I'm heroic."

Sophie continued to hold her hands balled into fists at her side. "Those scars consume you, but they are nothing to me. It's time you stopped staring at them, for it took me only a moment to look past them and see the man you really are." She took a deep breath, prepared to say more and then realized she'd said too much already.

She snapped her mouth shut and felt the heat of a blush creep into her cheeks. "My apologies. I had no right to speak to you that way."

She expected him to be furious, but when she dared meet his gaze, she saw that he was still grinning. "Wilkinson's little sister packs artillery. I had better learn to duck the cannonballs when she lets them fly."

Now all three of them were grinning at her.

Her cheeks were already hot, but they turned to crimson flames. "No… I would never…" She wanted to slink out of the room, but Lord Exmoor got to his feet and now stood before her to block her path.

He leaned on his cane with one hand and took her gently by the elbow with his other. "I am merely teasing you. In truth, it does my heart good to know you won't cringe whenever I come near."

Cringe?

She wished he'd stop using those words to describe himself. She was reveling in her good fortune and decidedly not viewing this arrangement as a necessary sacrifice to keep a roof over her head and food in her belly. Sophie knew of only one way to stop these ridiculous thoughts he had about himself, but speaking her mind was one thing. Kissing him was quite another.

Indeed, she wanted to stop his mouth with a kiss each time he was about to utter those horrid words about himself. But she dared not. He wanted a business arrangement and she would honor his wishes.

Did all his friends and family indulge his notions? Perhaps they were afraid to speak up and contradict him. Once she was his wife, she'd do her best to change his opinion of himself. It would be no easy task. The war had been hard on many men and too many had returned with their spirits broken, Lord Exmoor counted among them.

Even her brother had given in to despair at times. Most of the letters she'd received from him while he was on the Continent battling Napoleon were purposely cheerful and reassuring, but there were times when he could not hold back his sadness and the news he conveyed would reduce her to tears.

After reading those letters, she desperately wished to do something to help. Oh, she'd volunteered to assist the wounded soldiers who returned home, as many of the women of York did. But there was little else she could do. She couldn't wrap her arms around her brother. She couldn't comfort him when a friend had fallen in battle. She could only write to him of her daily routine and relate news of their friends and neighbors. In truth, he seemed to enjoy those letters most of all. "I'm sorry, my lord. I spoke out of turn."

He responded with a grunt and then ran his thumb lightly along her elbow. "No apology necessary."

Lydia cleared her throat. "Exmoor, I hope you don't mind but we must take your leave now. Sophie's gown is not yet finished and I'm certain you don't wish to have your bride sewing through the night and into the morning."

His eyebrow shot up in surprise. "Blast," he muttered under his breath, but Sophie was standing close enough to hear him. "I didn't think about your wedding gown. I ought to have made arrangements for a seamstress. I shall do so at once. What else do you need, Miss Wilkinson?"

"Nothing, my lord. The gown will be done in a few hours."

Lydia spoke up. "It's an apricot silk and quite beautiful. Your bride will look lovely wearing it, but it isn't enough. She has no suitable necklace or–"

Sophie gasped. "No, Lydia. It isn't necessary. I'll fashion something out of the scraps of silk."

She felt the squeeze of his fingers on her elbow. "You will not, Miss Wilkinson. The Exmoor pearls will be delivered to you in the morning. That is, unless you wish to take them with you now."

Her eyes rounded in surprise. "No, my lord. Truly, I couldn't ask this of you."

"You're not. I'm insisting." He glanced at his friends before returning his attention to her. "I ought to have thought of it myself. Seems I've been quite remiss, neglecting your wardrobe, neglecting the essentials, and yet expecting you to make a good impression on my family when I've done nothing to help."

He sighed as he released her to run a hand raggedly through his hair. A habit of his, she noted, whenever he was perplexed. "Once we're married, our first order of business shall be to have new gowns made for you. Indeed, an entire new wardrobe. I'll assign one of the maids to attend you, but if you'd prefer to select your own from my staff or interview suitable applicants for the position, that is your choice."

"I'm sure one of your staff will do quite nicely." Goodness, was she back in her dream? No, he was standing close and she could feel the heat of his body. She inhaled the light, intoxicating scent of musk on his neck and quite liked the subtle, but unmistakably masculine, scent.

She must have had the oddest expression on her face, for Lord Exmoor suddenly frowned and put his hand on her elbow once more, as though to support her. She wasn't going to swoon, although she was giddy and lightheaded. Last week, she was wondering where she would get her next meal. This week, her soon-to-be husband was insisting she acquire a new wardrobe, was insisting on providing her with expensive jewelry, and was about to hire a maid to attend to her.

Her life had certainly taken a strange turn.

An odd turn, indeed.

Sophie listened as the rest of the arrangements were made, but as she was about to leave with the Allworthys, Lord Exmoor held her back a moment. "Miss Wilkinson, I have a request of you. Rest assured, I will not ask it of you ever again."

She tipped her head in confusion. "Of course. What is it you need of me?"

"Gossip will be rampant, including among my family." He paused a moment, obviously not eager to explain further, but she smiled at him to urge him on. "I do not want their pity. I do not want them believing you are marrying me only for my wealth and title. In truth, I know you're not and I appreciate it more than I can say. But it would be most helpful to me if you… oh, blast… if you allowed me to kiss you once we've exchanged vows."

She nodded. "Ah, and you're asking me not to flinch when you lower your lips to mine."

"I was thinking to kiss you on the cheek. That's all. I wouldn't ask for more."

"No."

He frowned. "What?"

"No, I will not allow you to kiss me on the cheek." Honestly, if he didn't stop thinking of himself as ugly, she'd kick him in the shins. "But this is what I will permit you to do." She brazenly put her hands to the back of his head, and reached up on tiptoes as she drew him down for a kiss. She'd never kissed a man on the lips before and wasn't certain what to expect, certainly not the pleasant warmth that filled her the moment her lips met his.

Certainly not the *heat* that filled her as he circled his arm about her waist and drew her closer to take control of their kiss. Suddenly, she was pressed against his broad chest and found herself gripping his rock-hard shoulders to maintain her balance while he deepened the kiss until her mouth was deliciously crushed against his.

She kept her lips tightly pursed and closed her eyes to take in these new sensations, but she could somehow tell that his eyes were open and he was staring at her.

Didn't that make him cross-eyed?

He was laughing at her, too.

She felt the rumble of his chest and shoulders as he struggled not to laugh into her mouth.

She opened her eyes, intending to pull away, but he was having none of it. So as her eyes began to cross because they were standing too close and staring into each other's eyeballs, she saw the distinct gleam of amusement in his dark emerald depths.

She broke off their kiss and pushed away with a huff. "My lord, you miss my point entirely." She wondered if her face was as red as she believed it to be. No doubt, it was. Not a subtle rose or more obvious pink. Not even a light red. No, her entire face must be a deep, cherry red, deeper than a fiery red sky at sunset.

"And your point was?"

That the kiss felt awfully good. "That I do not find you repulsive. You are only repulsive in your own mind."

Oh, heavens! She was talking to an earl. No, berating an earl. What had she just done? She was penniless, homeless, and after instigating the kiss, Lord Exmoor would now believe she had no morals.

He allowed her to move away from him, his expression unreadable. Finally, he spoke. "I'm no longer a handsome man, Miss Wilkinson. It's obvious to all who knew me before the war started. But thank you for that ridiculously touching display. If this is how you respond whenever I anger you, then I think we shall get along quite well."

She cleared her throat. "Um, I didn't intend it to be quite so... passionate. I realize that I mustn't kiss you like that during our wedding ceremony."

He let out a throaty rumble of laughter. "Quite the opposite, Miss Wilkinson. I would greatly appreciate it if you did. I can think of no better way to quiet the gossips."

She thought on it a moment and then stuck her hand out in that same forthright manner she'd done yesterday. "Very well. We have a bargain. You may kiss me whenever you think it necessary at our wedding ceremony and our wedding breakfast. You didn't mention the breakfast, but I think it is logical that it should all count as one."

"Miss Wilkinson, we shall indeed have a good marriage if you seek to resolve our differences with that attitude. A very good marriage." However, his amusement seemed to fade away and he now sported a frown on his brow. "But there will be times when you and I disagree on a matter. There will be times when you disagree with others on a matter. I require little of you as my countess, but you will be my *countess*," he emphasized, "and as such, I will expect you to make your point using more discretion than you showed a few moments ago."

She shook her head in momentary confusion. "You mean my kiss?"

He nodded. "I understand you were merely making a point. A very enjoyable point. But you should not make a habit of it."

Sophie had hoped that she and Lord Exmoor might one day develop an easy rapport, but she now doubted they would ever be so fortunate. Not after that admonishment. She wasn't sorry she'd kissed him. Or sorry that she wished to kiss him again. "I don't make a habit of throwing myself at men, if that's what you're getting at. I'm not that sort of girl."

"I know." He was now rubbing the back of his neck. "It's obvious you've never been kissed before. I wish you had given me warning. I wouldn't have... hell, I have no idea what I would have done."

He stared at her, his expression revealing his consternation.

"My lord, what gave me away?" How could he know she was woefully inexperienced? Was her kiss so awkward? Lesson learned. She would not kiss him again. She'd just have to find another way to show him that he had worth. It wasn't a question of what others thought. This matter of thinking himself unattractive came from deep inside of him.

"Everything gave you away."

"Oh, I was hoping for specifics." She looked down at her toes, suddenly too humiliated to meet his gaze. "Then I suppose you've had a change of heart and won't kiss me tomorrow."

He reached out and gently ran his thumb across her lower lip. "You do know little about men. I'm quite determined to kiss you as often as possible. But you needn't worry, for all I require is a word from you and I shall stop. I have no intention of abusing your kindness."

She looked up, now thoroughly confused. "Good day, my lord. I shall see you tomorrow."

"I hope so, Sophie."

He hoped so? Did he believe she was going to call off the ceremony? Or was he the one thinking of calling it off?

CHAPTER 3

JAMES STOOD ON the steps of St. Paul's Cathedral struggling to control the rampant beating of his heart as Sophie stepped down from the Allworthy carriage and cast him a shy, but heartwarming, smile. "Good morning, my lord."

"Good morning, Sophie." *My Sophie.* He couldn't believe his good fortune, for not only had she shown up for their wedding, but actually seemed happy to be marrying him. Not for his wealth. Not for his title. He didn't wish to make too much of it. She'd gotten to know him through her brother's letters and felt as though she were marrying an old friend.

"Goodness," she said in awe, glancing skyward to take in the soaring dome. "This cathedral is beautiful." So was she. Indeed, to say that she looked beautiful was an understatement. The delicate silk of her gown somehow brought out the rose blush of her cheeks. The sun shone upon the lush strands of her hair, bringing out her magnificent auburn highlights. The Exmoor pearls glistened against her slender throat, and in that moment, James knew no other Exmoor countess had ever looked better wearing them.

He held out his arm to her. "Shall we go in, Sophie?"

She arched a soft eyebrow. "Yes... James."

He smiled as her hand lightly settled in the crook of his arm. The nearness of her body felt so good as they climbed the last few steps and slowly walked into the cathedral. She was subtly helping him balance himself, for he still struggled with stairs even when using his cane for support. "We'll have the ceremony first and I'll introduce you to my family during the wedding breakfast. Does that meet with your approval?"

"Yes, that sounds lovely." She tried to appear jovial, but gave herself away by nibbling her lip. "I suppose they all know about our arrangement. I hope they don't think I'm taking advantage of you."

Her cheek brushed against his shoulder as he bent closer. "It doesn't matter what they think now. In time, they'll come to know your worth as I do."

His words appeared to do little to reassure her, for she now gazed at him uncertainly. "Will you keep hold of my hand throughout the ceremony?"

He glanced at her hand still poised on his forearm and tensed. "Not if you don't wish it."

"You mistake my meaning. I want you to." She let out a shaky breath. "You see, my hands are trembling."

"Ah, I see. I won't let go of you." That he had no desire to ever let go of her was a problem he'd address at another time. It was his problem, after all. But not a consideration today. Sophie had agreed to behave like a young bride in love during the ceremony and wedding breakfast. His heart wished to take advantage, but his head warned that it was dangerous. He'd survived the war by thinking things through with intricate care and would survive this marriage arrangement similarly.

In any event, he dared not overdo it. No one would ever believe Sophie loved him.

Sophie was once again glancing at her slippered toes as they walked down the cathedral's center aisle. His family and the Allworthys were seated in the front pews leaving the rest of the vast cathedral empty. Perhaps the ceremony ought to have taken place in the privacy of the bishop's office or the rectory.

Too late now.

But it felt right to stand in front of the holy altar with Sophie.

James hadn't realized he'd been holding his breath throughout the ceremony until he released it when Sophie affirmed her vow with a quiet, but confident, "I do."

He turned to face her and saw that she'd already tilted her head upward in expectation of his kiss. What was unexpected was the soft glow of happiness in her eyes and in her smile. He'd have to thank her for that thoughtful gesture afterward.

He leaned on his cane with one hand, but placed his other against Sophie's cheek in order to better angle her lips to his. "Welcome to the family, Lady Exmoor." He kissed her lightly on the lips, counted to three… counted very slowly to three, and then ended the kiss.

She took a moment to open her eyes, but smiled when she did. "Thank you, my lord."

They were now married.

"Come, meet my family. They're eager to know more about you." Although his voice was even and matter of fact, he took a quick moment to give thanks to Sophie's brother. Harry may have wanted to save Sophie from a dismal fate, but in doing so, Harry may have also saved him. Too soon to tell, of course.

Sophie held on to his arm while he introduced her first to his dowager aunts, Lady Agatha Westwood and Lady Miranda Grayfell. Lady Agatha had two married daughters who were unable to make it to London on such short notice, but Lady Miranda and her four sons resided in London and were present.

James grinned as Sophie's eyes widened in surprise when his cousins rose and came forward to greet her. "Oh, goodness! You didn't tell me they were the size of gladiators," she said in an urgent whisper. "They're as big as you."

He introduced her to the eldest first and went down the line. Sophie nodded and repeated their names to better etch each one into her memory. "Viscount Grayfell," she said, about to bow, but James held her back. "You outrank Tynan. He bows to you. As do the rest of these scoundrels." But any attempt at formality quickly fell by the wayside as his cousins hugged him fiercely and in turn kissed Sophie on the cheek.

Introductions to his brother and sister were as informal, his sister, Gabrielle, rushing forward to hug Sophie, and his brother scooping her into his arms and twirling her around before setting her down and planting a wet kiss on her nose. "Enough, Rom. Sophie isn't one of your pets."

His brother, although not quite seventeen years old, was old enough to understand how to behave properly. "I know, but she's such an improvement over–"

James growled softly. "Romulus! You're not too big to have your ears boxed." In time, he might tell Sophie about Lady Bella Whitby, daughter of the Duke of Weymouth, the beauty who had once claimed his heart, but this was not the moment.

No, today was Sophie's day and he was quite proud of the way she'd handled herself up to now. His family could be intimidating, not only because of all the titles among them, but because of their imposing size. Even the women were tall.

Sophie, despite her average size, looked like the runt of the litter among them. A lovable runt, and it was no surprise that his entire family responded warmly to her. They would never have dared such familiarity with Lady Bella, for that proud beauty would have cut them at the knees with her cold stare.

That he'd once been in love with that Society jewel did not speak well of him, but it seemed like a lifetime ago. A time before he'd gone to fight Napoleon, a time before he'd engaged in desperate battles or faced biting cold, gut-gnawing hunger, and the foul stench of death. A time before he'd understood the importance of compassion and mercy, and the nobility in protecting the weak.

Yet, he'd still gone back to her upon his return from Waterloo. He wasn't certain why. Perhaps because he'd once been as proud and arrogant as Lady Bella and thought he needed to return to that life even though he was a changed man.

The first deep cut to his cheek had altered his life forever, and over the years, he'd acquired more deep cuts and more injuries, the most recent being his leg wound. He'd almost lost his leg and may yet if it didn't soon heal.

He shook out of his wayward thoughts. "Sophie," he said as they rode alone in his carriage to his townhouse to celebrate their wedding breakfast, "as Lady Exmoor, your place will be at the opposite end of the dining table from mine. But not today. You'll be seated next to me so that we may share our first meal together as husband and wife."

She nodded.

He noticed her hands were clasped and tensely resting on her lap. "I hope my family didn't offend you. They can be a bit much at times. My cousins and I are close as brothers, and they were obviously exuberant in my new found good fortune. It's obvious they approve of you."

She shook her head and laughed. "I'm not used to all this attention. They day is young and you may still live to regret your choice."

He leaned forward and covered her hands with his. "No, my sweet. I'm well pleased with our bargain. It's you I worry about."

She arched an eyebrow. "Why?"

He didn't need to say it. She had only to look at his unpleasant features to know the answer. His body was equally scarred, but she wasn't likely ever to see more than the scars marring his face.

The soft curls at the nape of her neck bobbed as she shook her head and sighed. "Ah, you're feeling sorry for yourself again, my lord."

He released her hands and frowned. "I'm only thinking of you."

"With all due respect, stop thinking so hard. Have I complained? Have I given you any reason to think I regret our marriage? I'll speak up for myself if and when I ever do."

He couldn't help but grin. "Very well, consider me duly chastened."

Those big brown eyes of hers, the rich color of winter chestnuts, widened. "I didn't mean to berate you. Please don't take my words–"

"I'm not angry, Sophie. In truth, I have a hard time reconciling your outward softness with your inner strength. You look like an angel, even more so now that you've adorned your hair with little more than a garland of flowers. It falls like a soft halo upon your head."

She touched a hand to her hair. "Oh, dear. Is it too much?"

"It's perfect. And I'm beginning to think that you are perfect, too. You know how to stand your ground. Softness and strength. It's a good combination."

She eased back and laughed mirthfully. "I hope you remember this conversation the next time I irritate you."

He grinned and nodded.

In truth, he knew he'd been given a gift in Sophie.

She was the one who'd gotten the lump of coal.

THE WEDDING BREAKFAST continued well into the evening, and Sophie could hardly keep her eyes open by the time the clock struck midnight. The guests were only now departing. Sophie hugged the Allworthys and the Exmoor aunts, Agatha and Miranda. She received warm kisses from his sister and young brother who'd imbibed too much champagne and was all giggles as she gave him a kiss on the cheek in return.

His gladiator cousins were the last to go and for a dreaded moment she feared they would settle into the study and drink the night away with her new husband. Had he asked them to stay? Well, she was having none of it.

Obviously, she and James were not going to share a traditional wedding night. But his family didn't have to know it. "My lord," she said, standing on the threshold of his study and staring at these five big men who proved her fears correct. They were indeed about to make themselves comfortable and drink themselves silly into the night. "I believe this is our night."

His cousins looked sheepish, but James looked stunned. "They know, Sophie. No need to–"

"What? Exercise my wifely rights?" Oh, dear! At first, they all looked like magnificent stags caught unaware by firelight and too dazed to move. In the next moment, they looked as though they were all about to erupt in laughter. Perhaps she ought not to have phrased it quite that way. She wasn't certain what those wifely rights entailed because her mother had died young and there had been no woman to explain such things to her. Lydia would have taken on the chore had she believed Sophie ever had a chance at a real marriage.

But these men knew what it meant even if she didn't.

Lord Grayfell, no longer bothering to smother his grin, grabbed his two youngest brothers by the scruff of their necks and motioned to the third brother to follow. "Let's go, gentlemen. You heard Lady Exmoor."

Sophie stepped aside as he approached dragging his brothers. Grayfell shoved the three young men out the door, but paused a moment to inspect her. "Thank you," he said quietly. "I think you're just the medicine my stubborn cousin needs."

The front door had barely slammed behind her when James strode toward her with a scowl as dark as coal. "I will never interfere with you and any of your guests again," she said in a rush. "But this is our wedding night and even if all of London believes that nothing will transpire, it is none of their business. I think it's important for your sake that we keep them guessing."

He still looked angry. "Important for me?"

She nodded. "Certainly not for me. No one cares about me. If not for you, I'd be out in the streets begging for my next meal."

Her words seemed to startle him as though she'd slapped him. "Sophie," he said with an ache to his softening voice, "you have me now. You'll never want for anything."

"I know, my lord." She breathed a quiet sigh of relief.

"James."

She nodded. "James. You kick yourself hard enough. You don't need the rest of London kicking you as well. I give you my word of honor, I shall never interfere with your nightly engagements again."

She eased as the anger seemed to drain out of him. "But one other thing... James."

His emerald eyes began to darken once more. "What?"

"The thing is," she said, now wringing her hands in consternation. "The day was so rushed and this house is so big. I had no time to explore it. So, the thing is... where is my room? I know my belongings were brought over earlier, but I have no idea where your staff has put them or where I'm supposed to be."

CHAPTER 4

JAMES CURSED HIMSELF for an idiot. "Your rooms?"

"Do you mean I'm to have more than one?" Her lips were pink and lightly swollen, and there was a sensual slant to her eyes because she was fatigued. He yearned to take the pins from her lustrous hair and watch the silken mane slowly cascade over her shoulders in undulating waves. She let out her breath and he caught the scent of champagne and strawberries on her mouth.

He leaned closer, his big body almost pressing against her slight frame. "You're my countess. You have an entire suite of rooms next to mine." He cleared his throat. "There is no lock on our adjoining door, but I'll have one installed if you wish. In any event, I'll hold true to my word. I promised not to touch you."

She ran her tongue along her slightly parted lips. "Unless I wish it?"

He nodded, fascinated by her mouth and desperate to claim her lips in a deep and urgent, grinding kiss. It took all his military discipline to hold to his promise, for he'd never ached so badly to have a woman, not even Bella.

What was it about Wilkinson's little sister that so stirred him? She was his wife now. His outspoken and adorably tipsy wife. He wouldn't risk facing her disappointment when she sobered in the morning. No, even though he ached to have her in his arms, yearned to explore her delectable body and take her, any intimacy between them would have to wait until she'd fully regained her senses.

Of course, then she would recoil in disgust at the notion of their coupling.

He drew away. "Come, Sophie. I'll show you where they are."

Climbing the stairs together felt surprisingly intimate. In truth, it helped to ease his agony, for this was something they could do together nightly. Also, there was something quite soothing in her manner and in her touch. He didn't feel awkward struggling up the stairs on his injured leg while she was beside him, subtly assisting him and yet not making anything of the matter.

"You needn't hold on to me," he said once they'd climbed the stairs and were walking down the hall toward their rooms.

"I know." She kept her hand tucked in the crook of his arm, little realizing the dangerous effect her nearness was having on him. "But it comforts me. I'm not doing this out of gratitude or pity, but out of joy. Yesterday, I was a nobody surviving on the generosity of friends. Today, I'm the wife of the Earl of Exmoor. Today, the world is full of possibilities. Most of all, today I will – hopefully – spend the rest of my days with *you*. I'm happy about that, even if you're not."

He was quickly losing patience with this upstart young woman. He didn't want to be flattered or coddled. He just wanted to be left *alone* to sink into his bed *alone* and somehow manage to keep that beast growling inside of him from frightening the innocent girl with the force of his need for her. Once he was *alone*, he'd relieve that pent up need in the same hapless manner as every pimple-faced boy on the cusp of manhood managed to do. "You're happy, are you? We'll see how long that lasts."

She stepped in front of him and scowled. "It could last forever if you'd let it. Why do you insist on being downcast and miserable?"

"Who said I was miserable?" Indeed, the girl had quite a mouth on her, something Wilkinson neglected to mention about his sister.

She rolled her eyes. "May I speak plainly?"

"You're going to do it anyway, so please proceed." She was a demanding bit of goods, and despite currently being a thorn in his side, he had to admit that he was enjoying her presence. She had a gentle but determined way of kicking his arse, and if he believed in such things, he'd think she had been born a Roman general in an earlier life.

"I like you, my lord. In truth, I was in danger of falling in love with you before I'd ever met you."

He dismissed the notion at once. "What nonsense did your brother put in his letters?"

"It wasn't nonsense. I think I could like you very much if you'd give our marriage a chance to blossom. I understand the deal we struck had…" She swallowed hard and blushed. "The terms were for us to maintain a business relationship." She swallowed hard again and placed a hand on his chest. "But if it was for my benefit, what I mean to say…" Yet another hard swallow. "I am not averse to… the other sort of relationship. That is, if you are not averse to it either."

He understood the drift of her thoughts. He ached to bed her, wasn't it obvious? But she'd imbibed too much champagne and it was good to know that she was amorous when drunk, but he wasn't going to start off their marriage with regrets. He might take advantage of her amorous advances at another time, but not this evening. They hadn't been married a full day yet.

As for those feelings she supposedly had for him after reading her brother's letters, the harsh reality of what he was would soon sink in and wash away all hope of a love marriage.

He took her hand and led her into her elegant bedchamber, pleased when she emitted a soft gasp of delight. "This is yours, Sophie. The door on the left leads to your dressing room. The door on your right leads to my quarters." He kissed her politely on the forehead. "Perhaps another time, but not tonight. There's a bellpull beside your bed. Tug on it if you need anything and your maid will attend to it."

"I see." She stared at her toes as she nodded. "You needn't worry. I won't disturb you, my lord. No, indeed. You'll be quite safe from me."

He sighed. Was he making a mistake? By morning she would realize that what she felt was gratitude and nothing more. She'd be relieved not to awake in his arms, not to have to stare at his scarred face or look upon the rest of his scarred body. "Good night, Sophie. I usually take my breakfast at eight o'clock in the morning. You are most welcome to join me, but it isn't required. Sleep in, if you wish."

She shook her head. "I'm not one to laze in bed. I'll join you for breakfast. That is, if you don't mind."

He tucked a finger under her chin to lift her gaze to his. "I don't mind at all. This is your home now. You may come and go as you please. I would enjoy your company in the morning."

"Just not tonight. I understand." She stepped away to retrieve the sheer, white night rail and robe set out upon the rose silk counterpane. "Sweet dreams, my lord." She appeared ready to say more, but began to hiccup instead.

Gazing at her just now, James was overwhelmed by the urge to toss caution to the wind and take her to his bed, but he quickly tamped down the wayward notion. First, she was utterly inexperienced and *if* there was ever to be a first time, it would have to be gentle and cautious so as not to hurt her. Second, he'd somehow have to keep his mangled leg from view or she'd be retching into the chamber pot at the sight of it instead of eagerly joining him.

Hell and damnation, those visions of Sophie stretched out before him, her hair a riot of dark waves cascading down her back and splaying across his white sheets, would have to remain just that. Visions. Reckless fantasies that would never come to pass.

Her string of hiccups brought him back to the present and reminded him that Sophie had imbibed too much champagne. "Do you need assistance with your gown?"

"No. I'll manage as I've had to do all of my life." The retort was more wistful than snide. "I'll see you in the morning." She marched to his door and held it open for him, making no attempt to hide her thoughts. If he had no desire to stay, then she was eager to boot him out.

She hiccupped again.

Gad! What was wrong with him? Sophie Wilkinson was the prettiest thing this side of the Atlantic Ocean.

The prettiest thing on either side of any ocean.

That was the problem.

He cared about what she thought of him.

He cared and was too much of a coward to face her disappointment.

SOPHIE LEANED AGAINST the door separating her quarters from that of her husband's and emitted a ragged sigh. Then a sniffle. Then she allowed the tears to quietly roll down her cheeks. She'd made an utter fool of herself, offering James unrestrained access to her heart and body, and he'd rebuffed her.

Dratted inexperience!

She ought to have known better than to mistake tender regard for something more.

He'd been by her side all day, looking after her and making her feel quite special. She'd even caught him a time or two gazing at her with unmasked desire. Obviously, she had misunderstood. He respected her, but didn't want her in the way that a husband in love would want his wife. "Oh, Sophie. What have you gotten yourself into?"

She leaned her back against the closed door and idly surveyed her room. To say it was large and splendid, didn't do it justice. Everything from the oriental patterned silk carpet, to the canopied bed draped in rose silk, to the gold sconces and elegant sweep of curtains hanging from the tall windows, spoke of wealth and power. She'd never known such luxury and would gladly trade it in for a husband who loved her and wanted to fall asleep with her wrapped in his arms. "Stop dreaming, Sophie. Be content with your lot."

She slipped out of her wedding gown and carefully set it in her massive armoire, which was vast and empty since she hadn't the clothes to fill it. Sighing, she donned her night rail and hopped into bed, glad that her maid had thought to put a hot stone between the sheets to warm them. Of course, she would have loved to be warmed by the heat of her husband's body.

No.

She had to stop thinking of James that way.

So she tried to banish him from her thoughts as she lay her head upon the pillow, but that didn't work at all, so she drew one of the many soft pillows strewn across the headboard against herself and pretended he was beside her and she was nestled against his broad chest. Much better. She immediately fell into a deep, exhausted sleep.

Sometime in the middle of the night, her sleep was disturbed by the sound of sharp cries that sounded like someone was in pain. Immediately thinking of James, she drew aside her covers and rose to investigate. The sounds continued as she reached the door separating their bedchambers, so she took a deep breath, opened it, and stole in.

The fire in his grate cast enough light so that she could see the shadow of James lying on his massive bed. He was thrashing in his sleep, the covers appearing to be caught around his injured leg. She crept closer and stifled a gasp when she realized he was unclothed. Then stifled another gasp as she studied the hard, muscled planes and magnificent contours of his body outlined in the dim light.

What would he do if he caught her gaping at him?

She forced herself to stop staring at him and wishing for things that would never be. Instead, she got down to business, carefully unwrapping the coil of bed linens around his leg and tucking the covers over him, for his skin was cold to the touch and exposure to the chill night air could not be good for his injury.

She returned to her chamber and quietly shut the door between them. She shivered as well, for the fire in her grate had died out and she was standing in her bare feet. Hearing nothing more, and hoping James had fallen into a gentler slumber, she returned to her bed. "Just a bad dream," she muttered, still worrying about how James had thrashed and cried out as though struggling against something dire. Knowing there was nothing she could do for him tonight, she fell into a restless sleep.

She awoke shortly after dawn to the sound of soft footsteps crossing her room. She opened her eyes and saw a pretty young woman with bright copper curls sticking out from under her mob cap moving about the room. First, the young woman drew the drapes aside to allow sunlight to filter in, and then she lit a fire in the hearth. Ah, her new maid.

Sophie sat up and smiled at her. "Good morning."

The young woman turned to her with a start. "Good morning, m'lady. I didn't mean to wake you."

Sophie set aside her covers and walked toward the warming fire. "You didn't. I rarely sleep in. What's your name?"

"I'm Bessie, m'lady." She gave a quick curtsy.

"Nice to meet you, Bessie. Do you know if his lordship is awake yet?"

The girl cast her a knowing smile. Obviously, she thought James had performed his husbandly duties last night, which he hadn't and wasn't ever going to do, but it was no one's business what went on between them. Or rather, what failed to go on between them. "Yes, m'lady. He's downstairs having his breakfast." Bessie's grin broadened. "He said not to wake you because you were likely exhausted."

"No, I'm quite refreshed this morning."

Bessie put a hand to her mouth and giggled. "I'm glad to hear it, m'lady. A husband ought to attend to his duties, that's what I say."

Sophie groaned inwardly. What had she said or done to give the girl the impression that she and James had spent the night together? Well, it didn't matter. The staff would find out soon enough that there would be no visits, discreet or otherwise, to her quarters by the man who had vowed to honor her as his wife.

Bessie helped her to wash and dress – even her best gown, a dark green merino wool – paled beside the grandeur of her bedchamber. She slipped the gown on and then sat on her bed in order to put on her comfortable boots and lace them. There was no help for it, she'd have to make do until she acquired a new wardrobe and elegant accessories to accommodate her elevated station in life. Goodness! She was now a countess.

She still felt like Sophie Wilkinson from York.

"I could polish them a little to cover the scuffs," Bessie offered, pointing to the boots.

"Thank you, Bessie." She handed them over. "Do whatever you can. I'll wear these in the meantime." She slipped her feet into her fancy wedding shoes, their soft apricot color a hideous clash against the dark green of her gown, but there were no guests about to care.

She patted the soft chignon Bessie had styled for her, and then glanced into the mirror and lightly pinched her cheeks. She hurried downstairs, hoping she wasn't too late to join James... perhaps she ought to think of him as Exmoor now. Yes, Exmoor was more formal and distant. Exmoor had abandoned her last night.

James would never have done so.

She paused a moment at the foot of the stairs to take a deep, confident breath, and then walked into the breakfast room with her head held high and her disposition unaffectedly casual.

James... no, he was distant and aloof Exmoor now... glanced up from his newspaper. "Sophie," he said with a genuine smile, setting aside the paper. He rose with a masculine grace, reminding her just how handsome a man he truly was. "How did you sleep last night?"

"Peacefully. And you, my lord?" In truth, he appeared clear-eyed and well rested. Had she imagined hearing cries of pain coming from his room in the middle of the night? Had she imagined creeping in to fix his covers? It seemed like a distant dream now.

"As well as ever. Are you hungry?" He motioned to the elegant fruitwood buffet that ran across the length of one wall and pointed to the silver trays on it. "Eggs, kippers, boiled tomatoes, scones, ham–"

"All this just for the two of us?" She shook her head and laughed. "I'll quickly grow as big as this house if I eat even half of what's set out."

He grinned as he held out the seat beside him. "Feel free to instruct our cook. But she's a testy old bat and carries a big rolling pin, so I would say nothing unless you wish to take your life into your hands."

Sophie let out a merry laugh. "Thank you for the warning. I think my first decision as Lady Exmoor shall be to allow Cook to do as she pleases. How's that?"

"An excellent choice." Although he'd obviously finished his breakfast, he motioned for one of the footmen to pour him another cup of coffee. He eased back in his chair and watched her as she ate her eggs and kippers. "What's your plan for today, Sophie?"

She set down her fork and turned to him. "I hadn't given it much thought. What do countesses usually do?"

"I'm not sure. They fuss a lot, but you're not the fussy sort. They host afternoon parties and belong to charitable organizations, but I think that your first order of business ought to be acquiring your new wardrobe. I've asked my sister for recommendations and she says that Madame de Bressard is the modiste used by all the best ladies, so I think we must send word to her and make an appointment at her earliest availability. Preferably today."

Sophie shook her head and laughed. "Are my clothes that awful? Oh, don't answer that. I know they are. Will you come with me to help me choose fabrics and styles?"

He winced. "Must I?"

She stifled her disappointment. "No, of course not. I wouldn't dream of imposing on you." She poked a kipper and shoveled it into her mouth.

"It isn't so much an imposition as a sense that I would be useless in such matters. One gown is the same as another to me, and the only reason I'm eager to provide you with a new wardrobe is that others will judge you by the clothes you wear. It's about them, not me."

She dabbed at her mouth with her napkin. "Ah, so you don't care what I wear... or if I wear nothing at all."

He sighed and leaned closer. "You're still overset about our... sleeping arrangements last night, aren't you?"

So what if she was?

She tipped her chin up in dismissal. "I don't know what you're talking about."

He cast her the softest smile. "Yes, you do. I wanted you, Sophie. But I have never taken advantage of a woman when she's drunk."

She gasped. "I wasn't... well not all that... were you counting my drinks?"

"No, not intentionally. But I know you had at least six glasses of champagne. We all did."

Her eyes widened. "No."

"It could have been more." He was still leaning close so that she could feel the heat of his body and inhale the subtle scent of musk on him. Was there something in that scent that made a woman want to claw at a man's body and rip the clothes off him, because she was feeling that hot urge at this very moment?

"So are you suggesting that if I were sober and asked you to... you know... that you'd accept?" She set down her fork and stopped eating, for her heart was beginning to beat excitedly and she was no longer hungry for food but for him.

He said nothing for the longest moment and Sophie thought he wasn't going to answer her question. She was about to turn away when he suddenly sighed again and said, "Yes. But I wish you'd give it more thought. It was never my intention to impose on you."

"I never intended it either, but something about *us* feels inevitably right. I don't understand it yet, but I know this feeling isn't about pity or gratitude. I tingle when I'm close to you. Only something deep and heartfelt would evoke that response in me. Do you think my brother was purposely matchmaking? Do you think he sensed we were a good fit?"

James snorted. "Nonsense, he saw me at my worst. We endured cold, hunger, and the most depraved conditions. We rarely bathed, rarely ate food fit to be consumed, and never knew whether we'd survive beyond the next few minutes. I hardly think the Marriage Mart was on his mind."

She wasn't quite convinced, for she and her brother had always looked out for each other. She felt a jolt to her heart, realizing that her brother had been thinking of her future even while taking his last, gasping breaths. "Well, I suppose we shall never know now."

James put a hand over hers, his touch warm and consoling. "It doesn't matter. We're together now. From this day on, you will lack for nothing."

"You see, this is what I mean. You say the noblest things and sincerely mean them. My brother certainly chose wisely for me, but I think he meant for us to share more than a business arrangement."

"Perhaps it was so before my injuries, but not afterward."

She saw that irritating sense of resignation wash over him and released a breath of exasperation. "There you go, hating yourself again. Please stop expecting me to feel repulsed by you, because I don't and never will. James, my room is quite large, too large for just one person to rattle around in it. I have no need for a big, empty chamber nor do I wish to climb into a big, empty bed each night. But I'd be content to share it with you."

"Sophie—"

"I'm sober now and I haven't changed my opinion. I understand what I'm asking of you. I know it would require an amendment to our agreement. I also know that this is something we must mutually agree upon. I won't press you on the matter. I just want to be clear about my hopes for this marriage."

"Hopes?" He laughed wryly and edged away. "You are an unusual girl."

"On the contrary, I'm quite traditional." She squirmed in her seat a moment, unsure whether to continue to press him about their marriage. It wasn't fair, really. He'd been up front about this business arrangement and she was already reneging on her part of the bargain. Still, it felt like the right thing to do. Her brother had been worried about her future, but he'd also been worried about James. Indeed, Harry must have purposely thrown them together to benefit both of them. "Will you change your mind and accompany me to Madame de Bressard's shop today? Assuming she will give me an appointment."

"I can't today. Truly, Sophie. I have a prior engagement that can't be rescheduled."

"Oh, I see." She shrugged her shoulders, pretending she didn't care, even though she cared deeply. There was something wonderful about being with James. She couldn't explain it, she just enjoyed being in his company. "Will it take you long?"

"No, not too long."

She waited for him to say more, hoping he might feel the same way about having her around and invite her to join him. But he said nothing. Indeed, when she hinted further, he ignored her to the point that he was being quite mysterious about this appointment of his. "What shall I do if Madame de Bressard isn't available? Would you mind if I visited the Allworthys while you're out?"

"Not at all. That's a nice idea."

"Would you drop me off there on your way to wherever you're going and then pick me up on your return home?"

He nodded. "Yes, it's on my way."

"Thank you, James." This was the first day of their honeymoon and she wanted to take advantage by spending as much time with him as he would allow. How else were they ever to get to know each other? She cast him a beaming smile. "It shall be our first excursion as husband and wife."

He cast her an indulgent, and slightly impatient, glance. "Sophie, it's merely a five minute carriage ride across the park."

She understood that she was making too much of it, but how else was she to convince him that they were meant to have more than a marriage of convenience? "It doesn't matter. We'll be together for that five minutes."

He shook his head and chuckled softly. "You're an odd little thing."

"No, I think I'm quite sensible. But I will admit to having opinions, and unfortunately, an inability to keep from stating them when I think they're important. Did you know that I helped tend the wounded soldiers at York's Royal Hospital?"

He arched an eyebrow. "That's a question, not an opinion."

She nodded. "But it's to let you know that I think your desire to hide your scars and leg injury from me is misguided. I understand that your wounds might be hideous, but those concern a patch of skin or a body part, not your brave and noble heart. That's the point I wish to make clear. If I wince or look away, it is because of my revulsion to the festering skin around your injury. Not of *you*."

His features remained expressionless. "Duly noted. And no, you may not go with me to my appointment."

She frowned at him, not bothering to mask her indignation. "I did not ask to go with you."

He squeezed her hand gently. "Yes, you did. Sophie, you are terrible at hiding your thoughts."

"Perhaps, but then you ought to see that I sincerely meant what I just said."

He nodded. "Even so, your good intentions are no less misguided simply because they're good. You will be repulsed. My leg isn't just a body part. It's a part of me. Part of what defines me. Let's put an end to this discussion. I'll hear no more of it. I mean it, Sophie. Do not bring it up again."

In truth, although his tone was gentle, there was an undercurrent of steely resolve and anger that she dared not stir up any more than she already had. "Very well, my lord."

"Good." He rose and left the table, leaving her to finish her breakfast alone. His limp appeared pronounced this morning and she didn't know if his leg was exceptionally sore or if he was simply doing it for effect.

She lingered over her coffee and ignored the rest of her breakfast, for she'd lost her appetite. Uncertain where James had disappeared to, and unwilling to disturb him, she rang for the Exmoor housekeeper to give her a tour of the house since James had neglected to do so. "Thank you, Mrs. Summerville," she said to the prim, older woman who moved about the house with the efficiency of a squirrel gathering nuts for the winter. The tour had taken a little over an hour and was quite helpful. "I can see the house is kept in excellent order."

Mrs. Summerville beamed, obviously quite proud of her work and pleased that Sophie appreciated it. "Shall I report to you each morning after your breakfast, m'lady?"

Sophie nodded. "That would be lovely."

After dismissing the older woman, she retired to the library and found a book to read for the remaining hours until midday. As it turned out, Madame de Bressard was available and agreed to an appointment for one o'clock that afternoon. Sophie suspected that James had outright bribed the sought after modiste, for Society's elite were lined up for her services and few were fortunate enough to see her on less than two weeks' notice.

Since James had his own prior engagement and could not stay with her, she invited Lydia Allworthy and Sophie Farthingale to meet her at the shop at the appointed hour. She and James rode there in his stylish carriage, but James said little and appeared distracted. She blamed herself for pressing him too hard on the matter of their marriage.

In truth, she was horrified by her brazenness. Married only one day and already making demands on a husband she hardly knew. But in her own defense, she felt as though their hearts had known each other for eternity. "You never mentioned where you were going," she said, hoping to engage him in conversation.

He had been gazing out the window, obviously lost in thought, but turned to her with a casual arch of his eyebrow. "It isn't important. Just a longstanding engagement. Stop asking me about it, Sophie. It isn't any of your business."

Why wouldn't he speak of it? Suddenly, she was struck with the reason. Of course! Oh, she'd been so stupid. He was going off to see another woman. Did he have a mistress? It would explain why he was being so mysterious about his so-called longstanding engagement. Her heart tightened, for she'd never considered that he already had a woman in his life.

Yet, he didn't seem the sort to maintain a liaison with... oh, dear. What if he did? What if this was the woman he loved? Sophie tamped down the urge to cry, for James was obviously irritated with her, and her turning into a watering pot would only make matters worse. How ridiculous she must have sounded to him, practically begging him to join her in her bed when he already had someone of his own choosing to fill that need.

She took a deep breath to calm herself, but how could she pretend it didn't hurt? "Shall I wait at the shop for you or return to Lydia's?" Could he hear the ache in her voice? Yet, she had no right to feel anything, for he'd been clear that their marriage was to be a business arrangement.

How long did he wish to remain in this other woman's company? An hour? Two? The entire day?

"I'll pick you up at the shop. As I mentioned earlier, this engagement won't take long." James descended the carriage with her and entered Madame de Bressard's shop to have a word with the modiste. "I want the best for my wife," he said, tossing Sophie a smile that had been missing from his features since their morning breakfast. "Lady Exmoor needs gowns for all occasions."

Sophie blushed, not only because of his outrageous generosity, but he'd called her his wife. She was, but it had sounded so natural and loving on his lips. Was she wrong about the reason for his pressing engagement? If it wasn't another woman, then why the secrecy?

He leaned close and kissed her cheek. "Have fun, Sophie. I'll have none of your Yorkshire frugality."

Despite her concerns, she laughed. "I'll do my best to spend you into the poorhouse."

She began to miss him even before the door closed behind him. Lydia Allworthy and Sophie Farthingale arrived soon afterward, and it was obvious they were well acquainted with Madame de Bressard, the pretty French woman who appeared to be in her mid-thirties. She had a quiet elegance about her and Sophie hoped that she might one day be considered just as elegant.

Inviting her two friends to help her select suitable gowns turned out to be an excellent idea. Sophie Farthingale had launched three daughters into Society and had excellent advice to give. Lydia was there mostly out of friendship and Sophie was warmed by her genuine affection. There was no stiffness or formality between them now that she was Countess Exmoor and she hoped there never would be.

Madame de Bressard's fashion sense was impeccable and Sophie left her shop feeling excited about her new wardrobe and eager for James to see her in these beautiful new gowns. The Exmoor carriage pulled up in front of the shop just as she finished the last of her fittings and was once more dressed. Her two friends kissed her goodbye and hurried off to do more shopping.

Sophie had enjoyed their company. However, she was eager to climb into the carriage and be alone with James. "I had such fun," she started to say, but to her surprise, the carriage was empty.

She turned to the driver. "Mr. Larkin, where is his lordship?" Her heart sank at the thought of James spending the entire day with his mysterious engagement and forgetting all about his new wife.

"I dropped 'im at 'ome first, m'lady."

She pursed her lips and frowned. "Thank you. Please take me home straight away." She was relieved that he would be waiting for her there, but why hadn't he simply stopped along the way to pick her up?

Sophie asked for him the moment she stepped into the entry hall and handed her cloak and gloves to Damson, the Exmoor head butler.

"He's in his study, m'lady. He wishes not to be disturbed."

She ignored the remark and marched straight into the study, quietly shutting the door behind her so that the servants would not overhear. "I had a lovely time at the shop," she said softly, her voice barely above a whisper.

James glanced up, but said nothing.

She was shocked by the dark, haunted look in his eyes, and noted the full glass of scotch in his one hand and the half empty bottle in his other. "What happened? I thought you were to pick me up from Madame de Bressard's shop." It took little brilliance to realize he was angry, disappointed... heartbroken, really. He had the look of a man in a torrent of pain.

She took the seat beside him and lifted the bottle out of his hand. "Please talk to me."

He frowned at her. "I asked not to be disturbed." As though to make his point, he drank the last of his scotch, draining the glass to the last drop and then tossing it into the fireplace. The delicate crystal shattered against the sooty bricks and melted into the blazing fire.

She'd already been assured he wasn't the sort of man to use his fists against a woman, but she didn't know him well enough to measure the extent of his control. He was in a terrible state, not just angry, but obviously frustrated and filled with despair. "James, you must tell me what is going on."

His eyes were a dark and angry emerald green, a dangerously turbulent green. "Must I? What right do you have to tell me what to do?"

"None at all." She stiffened her spine. "I'm only your wife. The woman with whom you exchanged vows a mere day ago."

"Right, and that does not give you the right to meddle in my life." A growl sprang from low in his throat. "I'll mourn my losses as I see fit, so get out and leave me alone."

"Your losses?" She shook her head in confusion. Had his mistress cast him out because he was now married? She knew little about the *demi-monde*, but this made no sense to her. Surely, the woman had to know he'd marry some day. "Are you in love with her?"

He squinted his eyes as he scowled at her. "In love? With whom?"

"The woman whose loss you seem to be mourning. I'm not sorry that your mistress broke it off with you, for I'm eager for our marriage to work out."

"You think this is about losing a bed partner?" He tossed back his head and roared with laughter. "I only wish it were so. No, Sophie. There's no one else but you. Soon, I won't have you either."

She gripped the edge of her seat. "What do you mean? James, I'm no wilting flower. Please, tell me what is going on."

"Very well, I shall." But the tone of his voice warned she wasn't going to like what he was about to say. "They want to amputate my leg. What do you say to that, Saint Sophie?"

She gasped. "What? Who told you this? Is this certain?"

"Stop asking questions. Just get out." He turned to reach for the bottle she'd taken out of his hands a few moments ago, but she set it farther away so that it was out of his reach.

"Stop drowning your sorrows long enough to talk to me." The sharpness of her voice brought him up short. He stopped reaching for the bottle and cast her a look of disgruntled surprise, one that revealed how eager he was to banish her from his sight forever. If he thought that a mere scowl would dissuade her, he was sadly mistaken. "Sophie Farthingale's brother-in-law is a brilliant doctor. The best in all of England, she claims. Lydia Allworthy agrees. So let's ask for his opinion. Perhaps there's something he can do to–"

"Stop, Sophie!" He ran a hand raggedly through his hair. "I don't need another doctor to tell me the obvious. The skin on my leg is dying. It's beginning to turn black. Do you understand what that means?"

She shuddered. "Oh, James! Yes, I understand what it means. All the more reason to see George Farthingale as soon as possible. I'll send a note to the Farthingale residence at once and insist that he come by today." She tried to remain strong for him, but even she was shivering and in despair over the news. "And if your leg can't be saved, then we'll still want the best doctor available to do whatever must be done."

"We? What a quaint notion? But this concerns me. What must be done is that my leg will be hacked off."

She nodded. "Perhaps."

"Stop it, Sophie. Your sunshine and roses attitude is grating on my nerves."

"Your wallowing in pity is grating on mine," she shot back.

His eyes rounded in surprise, and Sophie wasn't certain whether he would now strike her or laugh out loud. She wasn't going to wait to find out, so she pressed on. "I know it will be painful for you and I wish with all my heart that I could absorb some of that pain. Truly, James. I would do so without hesitation." Her lips quivered as she spoke and she feared that she'd soon burst into tears. "I promise you, I'll help in any way I can."

His expression softened. "What help can you be?"

"If this dreadful thing happens, your bandages will need changing. You'll be confined to your bed for a while, I suppose. You might need help with your bathing, feeding, someone to remain beside you should you become feverish."

"I have servants for that. Do you think I'd require my countess to perform these menial chores?"

Her fingers were still gripping the edge of her chair so tightly, her knuckles were turning white. "They aren't menial. They're important and if you think I'd allow anyone to take over those responsibilities, you're sadly mistaken. I will be by your side for as long as you need me... for as long as you want me."

He grunted softly, but his expression hardened once more. "Let me be clear about this. I don't want you."

She nodded. "You've made it quite clear. But why don't you want me? Because you don't want me to see you in a bad way? Because you don't want me to be overset by the messy operation or the fact that you'll now be missing a leg?" She took a deep breath and continued. "Because if you're thinking to protect me, I won't go along with it. But if you don't want me near you because you don't like me, then that's another matter altogether."

A tear dropped onto her cheek. Oh, dear. She was going to cry, after all. "Just tell me who you'd rather have by your side and I'll fetch that person. If you're to face this ordeal, then you ought to have those you love most beside you. That's most important."

He stared at her for a long moment, then groaned and reached out to wipe the tears streaming down her cheeks. His touch was surprisingly gentle. "Sophie, your noble sacrifice is unnecessary."

"It isn't noble. Nor is it a sacrifice. Life comes with burdens, so why can't we face them together? Even if we're to have only a business arrangement, then think of us as partners. Don't partners need to help each other out if they're to run a successful enterprise?" She sniffled. "As I said, if there's someone you prefer by your side, then tell me and I'll fetch her for–"

"Her? There's no one I'd rather have beside me than you. But that is neither here nor there. I don't want you beside me either. I don't want you to see me after the operation. I couldn't bear to see the revulsion on your face."

She wanted to grab him by his elegant lapels and shake him soundly. What did she have to do to prove that she ought to be by his side? "You never will. I promise you."

Although she still wished to shake sense into him, she reached out to place her hand upon his cheek. He caught her by the wrist. "I won't hold you to that promise. This isn't a simple matter of popping a boil."

"Really?" She arched her eyebrow. "I thought it was exactly the same thing."

He sighed. "I had no idea my wife was bossy *and* sarcastic."

"And willful. Stubborn. Unrelentingly determined. I'm sending for Dr. Farthingale. If he says it must come off, then we'll deal with the next step together." She rose to fetch a quill pen, ink, and writing paper. "No use protesting. I'm sending this note to him."

He emitted another soft growl, but she saw that his anger was fading. He wasn't pleased with her meddling, but appeared resigned to it now. "Just my luck, you were a Roman general in another life."

"One who must have loved you," she muttered.

He sat up in his chair and turned to face her. "What?"

Her heart shot into her throat. "Nothing."

"Did you just say that you loved me?" She saw a mix of amusement, horrified disbelief, and confusion in his gaze.

Too bad his ears weren't as mangled as his leg.

She grabbed the hastily written note and dashed out of the study with it.

CHAPTER 5

JAMES HELD HIS breath as George Farthingale examined the dark splotches on his leg. He tried not to wince each time the doctor probed along the bruised bones, but each touch caused a jolt of pain to shoot through his body, and the ordeal left him shaken and perspiring. This unwanted invasion was taking place in the privacy of his bedchamber, but the familiar surroundings gave him little comfort. "Well, Dr. Farthingale? What are your thoughts?"

George appeared to be in his late thirties and there was no mistaking the intelligence in his piercing blue eyes that obviously missed little. "Your leg is badly infected, but I think I can save it."

"Thank goodness," Sophie cried out softly. She had barged in as the examination was about to begin and insisted on remaining by his side even as he'd dropped his trousers, settled in one of the cushioned chairs beside the window, and suffered through the poking and prodding that the good doctor found necessary in order to determine the strength of his leg. "How can you save it?"

She continued to stare at his exposed leg.

If the sight of his infected, dying flesh didn't scare the little nuisance away, then James supposed nothing ever would.

"I have some powders that are quite effective, Lady Exmoor. They worked well on the men injured in the field of battle. But there are no guarantees. If my treatment works, then Lord Exmoor's leg might be healed. However, I can make no promises. The human body is a complex system. What succeeds with one person may have no effect whatsoever on another."

"You're military?" James asked, although he should not have been surprised. Dr. Farthingale was in fit condition and carried himself like a man who'd undergone the discipline unique to army training.

Dr. Farthingale nodded. "And had to amputate far too often for my liking. So let's do our best to save that leg of yours. I'll return tomorrow morning with those powders. Lady Exmoor, you'll see that he takes the doses I prescribe strictly according to my instructions, won't you?"

James laughed. "My wife may look soft and beautiful, but she has an iron will. Rest assured, she'll kick my arse if I dare protest."

Sophie's eyes rounded in dismay. "I'd do no such thing. I am not an ogre."

Dr. Farthingale smiled at her. "It's obvious, m'lady. I think your husband was only teasing you." He snapped his medical bag shut and bid farewell to both of them. "I'll see my own way out. I think the two of you must have much to discuss."

As the door closed behind them, James wondered what Sophie would do next. She'd put on a brave front for the doctor. Would she keep up the pretense now that they were alone? He watched her, saying nothing. After all, what could he say? He didn't want her help, but neither could he coldly dismiss her... not while he sat with his trousers down about his ankles and looking like a pathetic, sweaty mess.

Sophie sighed. It was a soft, breathy sigh that somehow touch his heart. It was the perfect mix of caring and strength. "James," she said, her voice achingly tender and at the same time, resolute, "shall I help you put on your pants?"

He laughed, for this was Sophie. Ever practical in the face of impending disaster. In truth, he liked that undefinable quality about her, that ability to make him feel comfortable under the most humiliating circumstances. She'd earlier admitted that she loved him. Did she mean it?

She couldn't possibly.

"No, Sophie. I'll manage that chore myself." He struggled to his feet, grateful that she made no move to assist him. Instead, she turned away and walked to the ewer filled with water that stood on his bureau and dipped her handkerchief in it. By the time she'd wrung out the excess moisture and returned with it, he had finished tucking in his shirt and buttoning his trousers.

She held out the damp cloth and he took it with a nod, wiping the sweat off his brow and neck. "Thank you."

She glanced at the wet, twisted handkerchief in his hand. "It's the least I could do. I know how irritating I can be at times. It is I who should thank you for indulging me."

He set aside the handkerchief and took her hands in his. "I think it is the other way around. I was behaving like a petulant child and you were the responsible adult who brought me back to my senses." He frowned. "I need to know the truth, Sophie. What you said earlier... did you mean it? Do you love me?" He knew it wasn't possible, but he was feeling rather low at the moment and needed to hear it from her lips, even if it was a lie. What could she possibly love about him? His sweat and the stale scent of scotch on his breath? His decaying leg and prominent scars? His disregard of all the small things that would make her life comfortable?

He hadn't done much other than buy her new clothes.

He'd been nothing but surly and rude in the little time he'd spent with her today. Blast, he hadn't even shown her this house. Last night, she'd had to ask him for directions to her bedchamber. "Never mind, you don't have to answer the question. I had no right to ask it."

"Are you afraid I'll lie to you out of pity?"

He laughed mirthlessly. "No, you're far too honest for that."

She smiled back, but hers was an openhearted smile that shone straight into his heart. "You mean, I'm far too blunt for that. I'm afraid I would never succeed as a diplomat." She swallowed hard and spoke into his chest, no longer daring to look up at him. "I do love you. If you'll indulge me for a moment, I'll tell you why."

He said nothing at first, for he was indeed curious. Stunned, frankly. "You've known me less than a week. Most of that time, I've been dismissive and curt."

"I've known you for years, James. You fought beside my brother for a very long time and his letters were filled with news of you." She placed her hand lightly on his chest, but still refused to meet his gaze. "I know it wasn't fair of my brother to force you to promise to marry me. I had every intention of releasing you from that wretched oath." She sighed. "And then you touched my hand, and my body began to tingle. If you must know, it tingles whenever we touch. It's doing so now."

He smiled, silently thanking whatever forces had conspired to bring Sophie into his life. He wanted to tuck a finger under her chin and tip her face upward so that she would meet his gaze, but he could tell by the rose blush on her cheeks that this admission was embarrassing for her, so he stayed quiet while she continued. "I knew from the very first moment that no other man would do for me. I was thinking only of myself when I went along with this ill-conceived arrangement."

He now tipped her chin up so that she met his gaze. "Not so, you did offer to let me out of it."

She shook her head and gave a groaning laugh. "You ought to know me better than that by now. If I had truly wanted to release you from your promise, we would not be married now."

He glanced down at her hand that was still resting upon his chest. "Are you still tingling?"

"Yes."

"Would you mind if I kissed you?"

"Not at all. I've been hoping you would ever since the doctor left us."

Was it truly possible she loved him, that she wanted him to kiss her? She was bright-eyed and sober. He wasn't, but so what? It was only a kiss. He wouldn't attempt more just now, for a man in his cups might think he was a brilliant lover, but in truth, he'd just be an incompetent, slobbering wretch.

His mouth closed over hers with all good intentions of keeping their kiss light and gentle, but the drunk part of him took over, the hungry, aching part of him that needed Sophie desperately and wanted to know all of her.

He pressed down on her mouth with little control and lots of abandon, teasing her pursed lips apart. He loved that she was too inexperienced to realize that one kissed one's grandmother on the cheek with pursed lips, but passionate kisses required something altogether different.

He deepened the kiss as he wrapped his arms around her and scooped her up against him so that he could feel the lushness of her body against his chest and inhale the lavender sweetness of her skin. All the while, he probed along the seam of her lips, gently forcing them apart with his tongue and plunging into her velvet warmth when she opened her mouth to gasp in surprise.

Probably one of the worst, sloppiest kisses he'd ever given a girl, but Sophie didn't seem to mind. No, she didn't seem to mind and at all, and was clutching his shoulders and winding her fingers in his hair with the same abandon as he was using to explore her delicate mouth.

"Oh, my!" Her words came out in a breathy moan. In the next moment, she pressed her mouth to his with the same desperately hot urgency that he now felt. "This is delightful," she mumbled into his mouth. "Why didn't you–"

"Sophie, stop talking."

He was still a little drunk. And limping. And sweating once more as he led her to his bed and settled atop her, knowing it was the worst thing he could do, but he would explode if he didn't have her soon. A volcanic heat was building up inside of him that needed to be released. He wasted no time in running his hands over Sophie's warm body. Blessed saints, her skin was soft as sweet cream.

He lifted onto his elbows, for his body was big and he had no wish to crush her. "I want you, Sophie." He didn't wait for a response before lowering his mouth to the pulse at the base of her neck and teasing a moan out of her.

He rolled aside, desperate to undress her, but she was tightly buttoned up and he was too overheated to manage those nefarious buttons right now.

His heart was pounding through his ears.

Sophie was reciprocating with her own explorations.

Someone was urgently pounding on his door.

What the devil?

The urgent pounding persisted. "James, I just heard! Open up!"

His cousin, Tynan.

James rolled off Sophie with a groan that sprang from the depths of his soul. "Bloody bad timing."

Sophie's hair was a delightful mess and her gown was hiked up to her thighs revealing those long, shapely legs he'd been caressing only a moment ago. She scrambled off the bed and hastily straightened her gown. "My hair's undone." She put a hand to her rosy cheek. "Is my face flushed?"

He grinned. "Red as a beet and your hair's tumbling down about your shoulders."

"Oh, dear!" She gave him a quick kiss on the lips that meant more to him than he could ever express, for it was an impulsive gesture that came straight from her heart. She muttered another "oh, dear" and fled to her quarters through the private door that separated their rooms.

Tynan once more pounded on his door with irritating persistence. "Answer me or I'll break it down!"

James donned his jacket, hoping it would cover the arousing effect Sophie had on him, and limped across his bedchamber to allow his cousin in. "What the hell is wrong with you? London had better be on fire or I'll–"

"I heard the news. Is it true? Dr. Foster wants to amputate?" Tynan grabbed him in a bear hug. "Ask anything of me. I'll do all I can to help."

James rolled his eyes the moment Tynan released him. "I'm fine, Ty. I promise."

His cousin frowned. "You are?" He studied him a long moment. "Well, I'll be damned. You are. I was worried about you. Needlessly, it seems."

"Well, you're here now. We may as well talk." James grabbed his cane and motioned for Tynan to follow him downstairs into his study. Tynan began to sniff the air the moment he marched in. "Reeks of scotch. What happened?"

James sank into the oversized leather chair he'd occupied before Sophie had marched in and kicked his arse. "Sophie happened." He grinned wryly and offered his cousin a seat. "She saw me wallowing in pity and bemoaning my dismal fate. She made it clear to me that she'd have none of it, so she grabbed the bottle out of my hand and held it out of my reach. I got angry and tossed my glass into the fire."

Tynan frowned. "Damn it, James. You must have scared her."

"Ha! If you must know, she scared the hell out of me. I was determined to drink myself into oblivion and was well on my way to doing so when she interrupted me. Another man might have struck her when she grabbed the bottle. I wouldn't have, of course. But she didn't know that."

Tynan nodded. "That was brave of her."

"In truth, if I'd dared raise a hand to her, she would have bludgeoned me with the heaviest object close at hand. She berated me for accepting my fate and forced me to see another doctor. Do you know George Farthingale?"

Tynan's eyes widened. "Never had the pleasure of meeting him. But yes, I've heard that he's the best around."

"That's what Sophie said and insisted on summoning him. He left here not an hour ago. Wouldn't get my hopes up, but he's going to try to save my leg."

"Well, I'll be damned. That's excellent news." Tynan eased back in his chair and let out a long, ragged breath. "Seems I needn't have worried about you, after all."

"There's no assurance his treatment will work. I may still lose my leg."

Tynan leaned forward. "Promise to let me know if that happens. I know what you went through in the war and how difficult this continued battle has been for you. Let me help in any way I can. Don't sink into the same abyss that seems to have claimed so many good men returning from the Continent."

James shook his head in acknowledgment. "Sophie won't let me so much as dip a toe into that abyss. She's quite something, Ty. I was sinking fast a few hours ago, but she pulled me right out of it. At least, for now."

"I'm pleased to hear it." He leaned forward and glanced around. "Where is she now?"

"Resting in her quarters." He cleared his throat, suddenly feeling the urge to laugh, for Tynan would be horrified to learn that he'd interrupted them in mid-pleasure with his well-intentioned concern. "She spent the day shopping with friends. As my countess, she'll need to look the part.

Not that I care. She looks splendid to me. But everyone thinks I'm fulfilling a debt of honor, that I've married a sad, little mouse. I'll not have them looking down their noses at Sophie. She has more worth than all of us."

Tynan choked on a laugh. "I'll be damned."

"Stop saying that."

"Can't help it. Didn't take you long to fall in love with her."

James frowned. "Who said I was in love with her?"

"You just did."

"I respect her. It isn't at all the same thing." That he coveted her body, that he craved her willing and responsive body with an ache bordering on madness, was irrelevant.

Tynan shrugged his shoulders. "Fine, keep deluding yourself. But if she happens to have a cousin who's anything like her, send her my way. I'm sick of these Society fribbles who giggle at everything I say and think I'm brilliant because I'm a wealthy viscount. Of course, I am witty and brilliant and wealthy, but that's beside the point."

They spoke a while longer, and although James still had Sophie foremost on his mind, he was also grateful for Tynan's friendship. He rose to escort his cousin to the front door when Sophie came downstairs. She glanced at James and blushed profusely.

Lord, the widgeon might as well have shouted out what they had been doing when Tynan interrupted them. Ty's eyes rounded in obvious surprise and he cast James a knowing grin. "Lady Exmoor, a pleasure to see you. Forgive my unexpected visit, but I'd heard distressing news and rushed right over to make certain my cousin was... well, I know now that he is in the best of hands. I'll see you both at my mother's party tomorrow evening."

James turned to Sophie the moment his cousin closed the front door behind him. "Care to pick up where we left off when Ty so rudely interrupted us?"

Her face turned bright as a cherry.

"Sophie, I'm teasing you," he said, caressing her warm cheek. "But I will visit you tonight, with your permission."

She released the breath she must have been holding. "Oh, thank goodness. Yes, you have my permission." Her smile was shy, but nonetheless enchanting.

He nodded. Perhaps he did love her, after all.

Even if she was a bossy bit of goods.

Yes, quite possible that he was falling in love with her.

CHAPTER 6

SOPHIE'S HEART WAS beating fast and butterflies fluttered in her stomach. After sharing a quiet supper with James, she'd gone upstairs and, with Bessie's assistance, readied herself for bed. She wore a lacy, rose nightgown, something she'd purchased today from Madame de Bressard's shop at the insistence of her two friends who'd claimed the color was becoming on her and matched the pale blush on her skin.

Her skin was a flaming red right now, for the lacy confection was quite skimpy. Nothing at all like her practical bedclothes. She'd insisted on braiding her hair over her maid's protests, as though having one's hair primly bound would lend propriety to what this evening would bring. "Why bother, m'lady? His lordship will only undo it the moment you're alone."

Assuming he joined her later.

She hoped he would, but he had much to consider regarding his medical situation. His leg had been painfully twinging this evening, so she wasn't certain what he would do.

She dismissed Bessie, and after the minutes passed with no indication that James was upstairs and preparing himself for their assignation, she was about to give up waiting and climb into bed when she heard the door to their adjoining chambers open. "Sophie?"

"I'm awake, James." She had been sitting in a chair beside the warming fire, but rose to walk to his side. He wore a black dressing gown that fell to his knees, and didn't appear to be wearing anything beneath it. He leaned on his cane for support, and although her gaze was mostly on his handsome face and rugged shoulders, she also noticed the muscular expanse of his chest and the sprinkle of fine, gold hairs across it as he strained to maintain his balance.

She glanced lower, unable to overlook the long, deep gashes that ran up the side of his injured leg, discoloring the skin from ankle to knee. Those gashes didn't end there, but his dressing gown covered the upper part of his leg, so the nasty gouges that existed beneath the fabric were hidden from view.

"You look beautiful," he said with a sense of wonder that immediately eased her fears.

Her smile broadened. "So do you."

He chuckled. "Hardly, but thank you anyway."

He said nothing more and conveyed how he felt by taking her into his arms and kissing her softly on the lips. He caressed her cheek and then ran his fingers through her hair to unbind her braid so that her dark, unruly mane tumbled down her back and curled about her hips.

Bessie was right.

She ought to have listened more carefully to the girl's advice.

In her own defense, she'd been too distracted to take in a single word.

James kissed her again, at the same time unlacing the front of her nightgown. Her heart shot into her throat, for she'd never experienced such intimacy before and didn't know what to do in response, or if she was supposed to do anything at all. Before she could ask, James began kissing her neck. She gasped as her body turned into a fiery inferno, his touch sending intensely hot ripples coursing through her body.

She gripped his shoulders and clung to him like a barnacle, afraid to let go. Her legs had turned to water and could no longer hold her up.

She moaned and gasped and cried out softly as the pleasurable sensations overwhelmed her. Finally, she closed her eyes and simply allowed herself to give in to the warmth of his lips on her skin and the excitement of his hands caressing her body. His hands were not those of a gentleman, not soft and milky, but unrefined as those of a workman. The roughness of his palms, coupled with the gentleness of his touch, intensified her response, stirred her passion beyond anything she'd ever experienced before.

In truth, this was her first experience with passion and she now understood what all the fuss was about.

"Sophie, let me look at you," he said in a groaning whisper.

She opened her eyes only to realize he'd slipped the nightgown off her body. She felt the cool air against her damp skin when he eased away, and ought to have been embarrassed standing before him without a stitch of clothing on. But he was staring at her in wonder, his smoldering gaze delighting her. This was her husband, the man with whom she would share the rest of her life, and she was pleased that he wanted to know her in this intimate way.

She rather liked the dark and fiery gleam in his eyes.

She smiled at him. "So much for business arrangements."

He chuckled and led her to the bed, but she sensed his disappointment in not being able to sweep her off her feet and carry her there. Any regrets were soon forgotten as she slipped between the sheets. James gently nudged her onto her back and settled over her, no doubt determined to take up where they'd left off earlier in the day.

A hot shiver ran through her as the rough silk of his dressing gown rubbed against her sensitive skin. She could feel the heat of his body through the fabric, but she wanted more. She wanted nothing between them.

She grew bold and attempted to unfasten his belt, not easily accomplished while her hands were shaking and she lay trapped between the mattress and his big, warm body. She loved the light crush of his weight upon her.

Her heart was now pounding so loudly, she was certain he could feel its *thud, thud, thud* against his chest.

He eased up on his elbows and cast her an appealingly wicked grin as she continued to fumble with his belt. "What are you doing?"

"Trying to get you out of your clothes." She sighed. "I'll need more practice."

"Indeed, you are delightfully inept at it." But he didn't assist her. Instead, he took her hands in one of his and held them over her head while he dipped his head and proceeded to place kisses about her.

Fiery sparks shot through her body with explosive delight. "Goodness, James!"

He showed her no mercy, kissing his way down her body and leaving a trail of fire in his wake.

"Stop!" she laughingly cried, aching to do the same to him. "I'm sure it's my turn, you wretched man." James released her hands and chuckled softly as he watched her tug at his belt with renewed determination. "It isn't funny. You've fastened a Gordian knot. How am I ever to get you out of your clothes?"

His humor quickly faded and his expression turned serious. "It isn't a pretty sight, Sophie."

Was he ashamed of the way he looked? She hadn't considered that, for he had a strong, lean body and a handsome face despite those deep scars carved into his cheek and jaw. "James," she said in a whisper filled with yearning, "it's part of you. Don't hide the bad from me. I want to know all of you."

He wasn't pleased, but after a moment, he nodded and rolled off her to remove his dressing gown. "Tug it this way and it slips right off."

Very well, he made it look easy. "I'll remember next time," she grumbled, and then all thought fled as she studied him in all of his splendor. No, he wasn't merely splendid. He was magnificent. Glorious. The flames glowing in the hearth cast a rich, golden sheen across his firm contours. She was able to make out the crisscross of scars along his back and several thin, red lines seemingly woven into the muscles of his arms. When he turned to face her, she saw more scars along his broad chest.

Her gaze met his. He wanted her as much as she wanted him. She glanced lower and saw just how badly mangled his leg was. A jolt shot through her heart, realizing in that moment how much pain he was silently enduring. His stoic silence only enhanced the nobility of his character. If she hadn't been in love with him yet, she certainly was now. She reached out her arms to invite him back to her, for she had an insatiable hunger for this man.

He was the handsomest she'd ever met, clothed or unclothed, and although she'd never seen any other unclothed before, she had viewed paintings of Greek and Roman gods and knew how beautiful a man's muscular form could be. James was that and more.

She ran her hands along his taut, corded muscles and sighed. He was her husband, and while he might not be in love with her, in this moment he certainly made her feel loved.

He kissed her on the lips and once more worked his way down her body, teasing and gently touching her everywhere, somehow knowing all her sensitive spots. These sensations were like nothing she'd ever felt before. Hot, exciting. Powerfully stirring to her heart.

Every part of her ached for his touch.

She began to soar amid the flames.

"Sophie, don't hold back," he said in a husky murmur.

Goodness, she was mindless and breathless and couldn't hold anything back, for his touch was magical. An intense, hot magic. All of her was on fire now, and she felt like a glowing ember floating upward to the sky. Higher. Ever higher. Then she soared, suddenly overcome by volcanic waves of pleasure that shuddered and coursed, hot and thick as molten lava, through her blood. "I love you, James."

He kissed her deeply on the lips and joined with her, at first with slow and gentle care, but soon he was a part of her, the two of them moving as one, as husband and wife. She was still that floating ember soaring skyward, only now the pleasure was even more exquisite because they were together. "James," she softly moaned, gripping his shoulders.

"I'm here, my love."

She ran her hands up and down his hot, damp body, memorizing every taut curve, every hard muscle. Every jagged scar. "I never knew it could be like this."

She loved the strain of his body and was fascinated by his movements. He seemed to move with the powerful grace of a dolphin cutting through the water. Each glide brought her along with him, a slow build of pressure, a climb to loftier heights.

Blissful.

Endless.

Timeless.

She felt the quiet roar of his passion, and she clung to his hard, muscled body as though he were her solid anchor in an uncharted sea. She loved this man so deeply. How was it possible when they'd only met a few days ago?

It seemed as though her heart had known him always.

They said nothing for the longest time, there didn't seem to be words necessary.

His caresses spoke volumes, and with each gentle touch, each light stroke, Sophie understood what he wished to convey. He hadn't said he loved her, but that was of no moment. The words would come in time.

He was a cautious man and not about to hand his heart over to her... not yet. Perhaps she more readily admitted her feelings for him because she'd read and reread all of Harry's letters dozens of times, letters that were full of mentions of James and his valor.

Had James ever poured over the letters she'd written to Harry? She doubted it.

James kissed her on the forehead to regain her attention, a quick, but exquisitely tender kiss. "Sophie, how do you feel?"

She smiled up at him and nestled closer to his big, warm body. He still held her wrapped in his arms. "Splendid. And you?"

"Humbled," he said after a long moment. "I never thought I'd have this. I'm beginning to think my injuries were a blessing in disguise."

She turned in his arms so that she was now facing him, but said nothing.

He ran his fingers through her hair, seeming to like the way it spilled over both of them in unbound waves. "Had I not been injured," he continued, his manner pensive and a light frown now upon his brow, "I would have returned home as cold and arrogant as I left. I would have found an excuse *not* to marry Wilkinson's little sister, probably found you a quaint, little cottage in the countryside and settled a goodly sum on you, then never given you another moment's thought."

"Oh."

He caressed her cheek, grazing his knuckles along her skin. "You were nothing but Smidge to me, just some girl who had been given a silly pet name by her brother. Not this beautiful Sophie now resting in my arms."

He kissed her on the lips before sharing the rest of his thoughts. "I would have continued with the usual round of elegant parties, settled on 'the right sort of girl,' a cold, proud Society diamond from a wealthy and noble family. A girl who knew which spoon to use for her *amuse-bouche*, and which gown to wear for afternoon tea... and which people to snub."

She gazed at him in dismay, realizing she would have been one of those snubbed. "Goodness, I'm glad I didn't know you back then. You must have been an insufferable clot."

He laughed as he caressed her cheek again. "The most insufferable in all of London. Everything changed for me after the war. I was angry and feeling awfully sorry for myself. I chose to honor my promise to your brother for all the wrong reasons. But being with you, well... you're good for me. You've opened my eyes to what truly matters. What's truly possible. I no longer want anyone else beside me."

No longer?

"Was there someone important to you before you met me?" Someone he would have married before the war, before his injuries. Sophie closed her eyes and tried to imagine the young lady who had captured his heart.

"I won't lie to you, Sophie. There was. You'll meet her at my aunt's dinner party."

SOPHIE SPENT THE hours before Lady Miranda Grayfell's party trying to shake off the impending sense of doom. Her gowns weren't ready yet and she had nothing suitable to wear. She couldn't borrow a gown from Lydia, for Lydia was too small, so her clothes would never fit. James' sister was too big, and how could she possibly ask her when they'd only met three days ago?

No, she had no choice but to wear the gown she'd worn to her wedding. It was the only one she owned that could pass for elegant. Madame de Bressard's designs were far more beautiful, but the first of them wouldn't be ready until tomorrow at the earliest.

Everyone who had been in attendance at their wedding would notice that she was wearing the same gown, but it couldn't be helped. Would Miranda or Agatha or Gabrielle pass a remark? They all seemed kind, however she hardly knew them. And what of Rom or the cousins? Assuming any of those men noticed. Still, it would take but an innocent slip of the tongue and all of London would know she was a fraud.

James put a hand lightly on her shoulder. "Sophie, you're woolgathering."

She turned to him. "What?"

He and Dr. Farthingale were now staring at her. The three of them were once more gathered in James' bedchamber, Dr. Farthingale having brought those promised powders. He'd just finished examining James to make certain there was no new damage to his leg since yesterday. "Lady Exmoor, perhaps I had better write down these instructions."

Sophie's eyes rounded in horror. He must have been giving her an explanation of the dosage to administer and she'd failed to listen to a word of it. Her face suffused with color, her cheeks burning in humiliation. "I'm so sorry. I was momentarily... distracted."

James regarded her with concern but said nothing.

Sophie began to wring her hands. "Please repeat your instructions, doctor. You have my full attention now."

"Very well." To her relief, Dr. Farthingale seemed not at all offended. The powders turned out to be more of a poultice that Sophie needed to prepare three times a day and very carefully spread wherever she noticed discoloration on James' leg.

"What do these powders contain?" she asked, watching intently as Dr. Farthingale prepared and then administered the poultice to show her how it was done. He then had her do the same under his watchful eye.

"I've read a little on ancient Celtic herbal lore," she said as she rubbed the foul-smelling concoction onto her husband's leg. "In the olden days, healers used to rub mushroom-like molds upon an open wound to stave off infection. These molds were found on the bark of decaying trees."

The doctor appeared to be impressed. "This poultice is similar, Lady Exmoor. During the war, I couldn't simply roam the forests in search of tree molds, for there were too many of Napoleon's soldiers lurking about. So I tried using a bread mold extract." He gave a short, wry laugh. "There was plenty of bad bread around. Stale, rotting with age, and dampened by the constant rain. Turns out, it worked remarkably well on the men injured on the battlefield."

"Brilliant," she said with a smile, suddenly realizing how foolish and insignificant her worries about a suitable gown were. "No wonder you're so well respected."

He sighed and shook his head. "You flatter me, Lady Exmoor. I wish I could work miracles and save everyone under my care, but it simply isn't possible. Fortunately, your husband is young and strong. He's likely to respond well to this treatment."

She wanted to ask him to please call her Sophie, but didn't know enough yet about the proper etiquette to mention it. She'd ask James later. She also wished to invite the Farthingales over for tea, but that would also have to wait until she and James were alone to discuss the matter.

Dr. Farthingale left soon after, but she remained in the bedchamber with James. He drew up his trousers and buttoned them while she busied herself washing the poultice off her hands. "Oh, dear. I still smell like old mold. I'll have to dip my hands in lemon later to remove the odor." She turned to James and rolled her eyes. "Your leg's smeared with it, and yet you still smell divine. It isn't fair."

He grinned. "I'm sure I reek. My aunt won't be pleased by the unpleasant odor that will follow me into her elegant salon. It'll put a damper on everyone's appetite. Well, almost everyone. My cousins can devour an entire boar in one sitting. That's just for starters. I doubt anything will interfere with their appetites."

He caught her up in his arms. "Speaking of food, you're a most tempting morsel. I could devour you right now, Sophie." He kissed her with a depth of feeling that surprised her.

Her heart was leaping and pounding, and her legs were wobbling so that she could hardly stand on her own by the time he ended the kiss. "My, that was nice."

"Dr. Farthingale may be brilliant," he said, his voice husky and filled with affection, "but you're the one who deserves all the credit if this leg of mine is saved."

He kissed her again, but when he released her and eased back, he didn't appear as cheerful as he had a moment earlier. "This poultice is to be applied to my leg at bedtime. I can't very well... no sense both of us holding our noses through the night. You won't be able to sleep with–"

Her eyes rounded in alarm. "Are you saying that you don't wish to share my bed?" She swallowed hard, struggling to tamp down her distress. "Didn't you enjoy last night?"

"Holy saints, yes! How could you think I didn't? Once this leg is healed, you won't be able to get me out of your bed." He rubbed a hand across the back of his neck. "I'm only thinking of your comfort."

Or was he thinking of the woman he truly wanted to marry. What would happen when he encountered his first love at Lady Miranda's dinner party? "That's it? No other reason than my comfort? Are you certain?"

He studied her expression and sighed. "What's wrong, Sophie? You've been distracted all day. Did *you* not enjoy last night?"

"You know I did. I think I was quite vocal about it." She blushed. "But James, I want to make a good impression on your friends and family, only... none of my new gowns are ready yet. All I have is the gown I made for our wedding."

"Blast," he said softly. "I've done it again. Been thoughtless, haven't I? But you're a beautiful woman, Sophie. You'll look perfect in any gown you wear."

"Everyone will know that it's the same one."

"The women perhaps. The men will simply notice the spectacular way you fill it out. I'll have to smash a few noses to keep the oglers in line, of course." He studied her a moment longer. "You're still fretting."

She nodded. "I don't want them to think less of me."

"My aunts and sister will never do that. Did they say anything to you to make you think otherwise?"

"No. They were the soul of kindness." She slipped out of his arms. "I've never been to an elegant dinner party before. Even if the gown passes muster, what about everything else I say or do? I don't wish to embarrass you. Especially in front of the woman you once loved."

Groaning, he arched a wicked eyebrow. "You're jealous. Well, if that isn't the topping on the cake. You think I'll take one look at Bella and realize my mistake in marrying you." He laughed heartily.

Bella? Even her name meant beautiful.

Sophie wasn't jealous, so much as scared.

Now that she'd fallen in love with James, she wasn't keen on losing him.

He tipped her chin up and forced her gaze to his. "Her name is Lady Bella Whitby and her father is the Duke of Weymouth. She's as haughty and proud as she is beautiful, and the greatest favor she ever did me was to turn me down."

"You proposed to her?" Sophie's heart sank into her toes. She hadn't realized the extent of his affection for this Society paragon.

"I did. The moment I returned from Waterloo."

"But that was only a few months ago." Could her heart sink any lower?

She didn't think it was possible.

"Two months ago, to be precise," he said, and her heart sank through the floor.

CHAPTER 7

JAMES GLANCED DOWN the dining table at Sophie, wishing Miranda had allowed them to be seated together, but it was never done that way at these fancy dinner parties. Husbands and wives were always separated. Sophie, in accordance with her rank, wound up seated beside his cousin, Tynan. He knew Ty would look out for her and subtly assist her through the intricacies of the silverware etiquette and any other frivolity that she had yet to master.

He'd given Sophie the Exmoor pearls to wear and they looked perfect resting against her slender throat. Their luster paled in comparison to the brilliance of her soft smiles, the smiles she cast his way whenever she caught him looking at her.

He did so quite often.

"Grayfell seems to be enjoying your wife's company," Bella said, for she'd been seated next to him. His aunt had warned him about the awkward seating arrangements and apologized profusely. At first, he'd thought it was a hoax. But it wasn't, and he was still quietly seething about the sordid twist of fate that had him placed by Bella's side.

Miranda should have ignored protocol this time and put him as far away from Bella as possible.

He turned to the arrogant beauty who had once claimed his heart, no longer feeling lesser because of his scars or the fact that she'd rejected his offer of marriage. "Why shouldn't Grayfell like her? She's charming and engaging. Everyone enjoys her company."

"But do you?" Bella obviously believed he was saddled with an unwanted wife, and found his predicament most amusing. "Really, Exmoor. I know you're making the best of a bad situation, but you needn't keep up the pretense with me."

He hadn't seen Bella since the day he'd proposed and she'd

immediately rejected him. The look of horror as she'd gazed at his scarred face was not one he'd soon forget. She'd almost tossed up her morning's kippers and eggs.

"It isn't a pretense." He'd proposed to Bella the moment his regiment – or what remained of it – had landed in England. After receiving her scathing rejection, he'd limped home, determined to hide away and lick his wounds. He didn't think his heart could ever ache worse. "I got the better part of the bargain."

He never expected to fall out of love with Bella.

Had he ever loved her? He didn't think so, but he had been caught up in all she represented; the admiration of the *ton* elite, the pride in courting an Incomparable, and upon his return from war, the desperate need to regain his former status and pretend he had not come back home damaged.

And he never expected the force of nature that was Sophie to storm into his life. He was counting his blessings, for she lightened his soul. She'd fought to save his leg.

Bella would have done nothing of the sort.

He stared down the table at Sophie again. "Indeed, I'm quite content with my bargain." He couldn't begin to explain the impact Sophie had wrought on his life or the joy he now felt whenever she was near. His thoughts drifted to last night and her passionate response when they'd coupled.

He couldn't wait to have her in his arms again.

She made him feel whole.

"Oh, how sweet." Bella pursed her lips in disdain. "But who else do you think will accept her? She's a woman with no connections. No family. No decent clothes. No training to be a countess. Take my advice and hide her somewhere in the countryside. If you keep her in London, she'll make you a laughingstock."

The spoonful of leek soup he'd just swallowed burned down his throat. "I'm most grateful for your concern."

She mistook his sarcasm for appreciation and cast him a condescending nod. "I'm only thinking of what's best for you, Exmoor."

And that was another thing he couldn't stand. Calling each other by their titles, something Bella always did, even during their most private moments. Those had occurred before he'd gone off to battle, before his scars and injured leg. Indeed, they'd shared intimacies for Bella had allowed him to take liberties. But moaning "Exmoor, Exmoor" didn't have quite the same sensual ring as Sophie's delicious whispers of his name while in the throes of ecstasy. *James. I love you, James.*

He couldn't wait to coax those breathy moans and passionate gasps from her sweet lips again tonight. "You needn't worry about me, Lady Bella. I'm more than all right."

"Good, because I know how badly I hurt you." She discreetly reached under the table and placed a hand on his good thigh. He would have been yelping and leaping out of his chair if she'd touched the other. "I've decided to accept the Duke of Bradshaw's offer of marriage. Perhaps you'll attend the wedding now that you and I are friends once more."

Her fingers edged upward– "What are you doing?" He grabbed her hand and jerked it away. "I repulse you. Or have you forgotten?"

Her lips pursed in a practiced pout. "There's a brutish quality about you with those scars. I will admit that I was quite taken aback at first. Perhaps I was a bit hasty."

"No, you were right."

She quirked her head in confusion. "Oh, you mean because of your leg? I understand that Dr. Farthingale is going to save it."

"He'll try. It may still have to come off."

She made no attempt to hide her disgust. "I see. That would be a problem."

He arched an eyebrow. "A problem for me, but you have nothing to do with my life now. You needn't concern yourself with how many of my body parts will have to be hacked off."

The look of revulsion never left her eyes. "Do you mean to say that you might lose more than your leg?"

"Yes. Most definitely." He was talking about his heart.

The heart that he was quickly losing to Sophie.

He'd been a fool to hold back. What had he hoped for? A torrid affair with Bella? A quiet annulment – hell, too late for that – from his marriage to Sophie? A damn business arrangement that would leave him free to pursue discreet liaisons with any woman who caught his fancy?

Sophie had been in his life only a few days.

He couldn't imagine his life without her.

"LADY EXMOOR," TYNAN said, following Sophie's gaze as she watched yet another exchange between James and Bella, one that was obviously private and intimate, for their bodies were turned toward each other so that the dinner guests seated on the other side of each of them were shut out. "You needn't be concerned."

But the pity in his eyes revealed that she ought to be.

"I'm not," she tried to assure him, however the water gathering in her eyes and threatening to spill onto her cheeks obviously failed to convince him. She set down her fork, the trout floating in a cream sauce having no appeal. "It's only that... I didn't realize... she's so beautiful."

He shrugged. "She certainly thinks so."

Sophie laughed despite her dismay. "Don't you also think so? Obviously, she is."

"Yes, she's spectacular." He shrugged again. "But I doubt there is a man seated at this table who would choose her over you."

Now she laughed with genuine mirth. "Thank you, Lord Grayfell. You're an atrocious liar, but it's most appreciated."

He glanced down the table once more and then turned to her. "The ladies will retire to my mother's parlor while we men have our drinks in the study. Bella will use the opportunity to sink her claws into you." He paused a moment as though to emphasize his point. "She will certainly attempt to insult you, mark my words. You're not experienced enough to handle her. If she tries anything, don't respond. Seek out my mother."

"Are you suggesting that I hide behind your mother's petticoats?" She frowned. "Am I to let others fight my battles?"

His eyes widened in surprise. "My cousin said you were a Roman general in an earlier life." He shook his head and laughed. "He appears to be right. However, I still must caution you. Lady Bella isn't above fighting dirty. She has mastered the art of politely shredding one to ribbons and won't go easy on you. Have a care. James was once hers and she isn't quite ready to give him up."

"I know he loved her." Perhaps he still did. "But she refused his proposal."

"She doesn't want him, mind you. But neither does she want you to have him. Promise me that you'll let my mother deal with her."

"And what if Lady Bella insults her?"

"She won't dare, for my mother's too powerful. But you're viewed as weak prey. Have you ever seen a wolf tear apart an innocent lamb? It isn't pretty."

Sophie's heart was firmly lodged in her throat by the time the ladies walked into Lady Miranda's salon. To her relief, Gabrielle and Lydia quickly came to her side, so the three of them sat together. Still, it wasn't enough to dissuade Lady Bella. She stood beside the window with her own friends, speaking loud enough to be heard by all in the room.

"Exmoor can't wait to be rid of her. Sad little thing, he told me that he intends to send her packing once his leg heals."

Sophie breathed a sigh of relief. Was this the worst Bella could do?

Gabrielle patted her arm. "Ignore that witch. I never liked her. I'm glad James is now rid of her. She's the one he ought to have sent packing years ago." She kept hold of Sophie's arm. "James told me what you did for him regarding his leg."

Sophie blushed. "I did nothing but recommend Dr. Farthingale. We're hopeful, but there are no assurances."

Lydia nodded. "Yes, that's what you've brought him. Hope. That gift is priceless."

Gabrielle heartily agreed.

Bella must have heard them speaking, for there was an undercurrent of menace in her laughter. She started toward them, her minions following at her heels, for Sophie didn't know what else to call these so-called elegant ladies who trailed after her like sheep. "Exmoor obviously didn't bother to tell you the rest of it. Poor man, he confided in me that his leg wasn't the only part of him in danger of being lost."

Sophie shook her head, momentarily confused. She'd been in his chamber during the doctor's examination and would have known if something else was going on.

"Oh, you don't know? Well, I suppose there's no reason he would confide in you. It's obvious that you mean nothing to him. Most embarrassing for you." She turned to her friends, no longer paying Sophie any notice. "He begged me to take him back. I had to put him in his place. After all, I've moved on and will soon be married."

Sophie curled her hands into fists. What utter rot! Perhaps James did care for the beauty and want her back, but he wasn't the sort ever to beg. He had too much pride. What troubled her was the possibility that he was more badly injured than he'd let on. But why spare her the bad news? And why tell Bella? That made no sense at all.

What had she overlooked about his health? His arms were scarred, but those scars had healed. Hadn't they?

She rose as the gentlemen joined them and servants began to set out tables for Lady Miranda's guests to play cards. She didn't know how to play. Her evenings in York were usually spent writing letters or quietly reading. She hadn't attended any assemblies since her brother had gone to war, so she didn't know the latest dances either.

She noticed James walk in, his limp worse than usual. She tried to mask her worry, but she wasn't very good at hiding her feelings. James immediately noticed that something was wrong. "Did Bella say something to you?"

He frowned and glanced over her shoulder toward where Bella stood.

Sophie nodded and began to wring her hands. "She said your leg wasn't the only part of your body that you were in danger of losing. Is there something else you haven't told me? Not that I wish to pry, but... oh, dear. I can't help fretting. Whatever it is, James, I'll help you. I wish you'd tell me what it is."

His expression lightened and he laughed softly. "Don't worry about me, Sophie. There is something, but I can't tell you here."

She nibbled her lip. "Oh, dear. Then it truly is something serious. But why are you smiling?"

His response was cut short when Bella called to him from her seat at one of the card tables. "Exmoor, come make up our fourth for whist. You must partner me or else Lady Miranda and Lord Grayfell shall have no competition. Come, leave your wife and join me."

"Leave my wife," he muttered under his breath so that only Sophie heard. "Now that's a loaded comment, if I ever heard one. What do you think, Sophie? Shall I leave you?" He gave her elbow a little squeeze. "I think not," he said quietly, arching an eyebrow to convey his amusement. "I'd much rather take our leave so that you may slather that foul poultice on my leg and then allow me to make mad, passionate love to you."

She shook her head and grinned at him. "How can I resist that tempting offer? But if we are to make love, we ought to do it with clothes pins on our noses."

He laughed.

"Exmoor!" Bella pushed back her chair so that it made a scraping sound against the polished wood floor as she stood up with marked annoyance. She looked quite determined, drumming her fingers on the card table and glowering at him. "You're delaying the game. Leave your wife and join me."

He led Sophie to where Bella stood with her chin proudly tilted upward. Tynan was already on his feet as they approached. His gaze swept from James to Bella and finally rested on Sophie.

He appeared poised for battle.

Goodness, she didn't need Grayfell, as well meaning as his intentions were, to intercede on her behalf. The fewer parties involved the better, for she had no wish for this dinner party to descend into a brawl.

To everyone's surprise, James ignored Bella and turned to his aunt. "Miranda, forgive me. Lady Exmoor and I must take our leave. It's been a long day for both of us."

Bella was having none of it. "How noble of you, Exmoor. But you needn't keep up the pretense among friends. We all know why you married her. We all know that she came to you with nothing. No clothes, not a shilling to her name. No family."

His expression darkened. "Enough, Bella. You're making a fool of yourself."

"Me?" She tossed back her perfect golden curls and sneered. "You're the fool, believing I'd ever have you." She turned to Sophie. "He only married you because I refused him."

Sophie nodded. "I'm well aware and am most grateful for your bad judgement."

Bella gasped. "Exmoor, will you allow your wife to speak to me that way?"

"The more pertinent question is, will I allow you ever to mock my wife or treat her with less than utmost respect? The answer to that is no." He made no attempt to mask his anger, and Sophie wasn't certain whether she ought to be cheering or trying to stop him before he lost all his friends.

It was one thing for her to be snubbed, but she didn't wish to be the cause of his banishment from Society. He ignored the gasps and glares he was receiving from Bella's minions and continued. "As for that rubbish about shipping Sophie out of London, rest assured, it is utter nonsense and will never happen."

He now turned to Sophie, his expression blatantly tender and loving. "I'm honored to have you as my wife and want nothing better than to keep you by my side for always."

Sophie placed her hand lightly on his forearm. "I shall be. Always." She hoped her smile in response conveyed the depth of her love for him.

Bella emitted a sound from her lips that sounded remarkably like a hiss. "We'll see how long she'll stay around when your next limb is hacked off. There'll be little of you left to love."

Had she a battle axe, Sophie would have cleaved the wretched woman in half. But she was more distressed about James' other injuries. How could she have forgotten about them? She squeezed his arm to assure him that she would keep to her word. "You know it isn't so. I'll love you no matter what happens. A limb does not define you. It's only the heart that matters. You have my heart and will always have it."

He covered her hand with his. "I know, my love."

Her eyes rounded in surprise and she gaped at him. My love? Of course, he must have said it for show. He couldn't possibly mean...

goodness, he was looking at her as though he did mean precisely those words.

"Lady Exmoor," he said with a devilish grin. "*My* lady. *My* love. Since Lady Bella has so thoughtfully raised the matter of the body part I am next in danger of losing, I may as well tell you what it is." He turned to face the other guests, all of whom were now buzzing around them, but they immediately quieted and fell silent in expectation of his next words. "I may as well tell all of you, for I won't be able to keep it a secret much longer."

Sophie felt bereft. Tears welled in her eyes. Was he dying and had wanted to keep the news even from her?

He tucked a finger under her chin and tilted her face upward to kiss her lightly on the lips. Kissing one's wife at a fashionable party? Was such a thing ever done? She meant to speak up, but his expression stilled her words. "It is my heart, Sophie."

"Your heart is failing?" She couldn't bear it. "What did Dr. Farthingale tell you? How long do you have to live?"

He laughed softly. "No, you misunderstand. It isn't failing. I'll live another fifty years, I hope. It is my heart that I'm *losing*... to you. That fragile organ was crushed by time and circumstances until you came along and revived it." He kissed her again, this time with a deep and abiding reverence. "I love you."

How was a countess to behave when the man she loved to the depths of her soul apparently loved her back? She grabbed him by the lapels and raised on tiptoes to kiss him back in a fervent and thoroughly inappropriate manner. "You're still crying," he said, noticing the tears on her cheeks which were impossible to overlook.

"Happy tears."

"I do love you, Sophie." He wasted no time in taking her home and showing her just how much.

He showed her through the night.

He showed her before she rubbed the poultice on his leg and afterward.

"James," she said, waking at the break of dawn to find herself alone in her large bed, the crumpled sheet and lingering warmth being the only trace that James had been beside her. She sat up and glanced around, surprised to find him standing by the window, gazing outward into the garden.

He'd drawn back the drapes so that rays of sunlight filtered into her bedchamber and brightened it. He stood there in his God-given beauty, wrapped in golden sunlight, as she walked to his side.

"I didn't mean to wake you." He drew her up against his warm body so that her back nestled against his chest. "I used to watch the sun come up every morning while I was on the Continent. The sunrise was significant, for it meant I'd survived another day of battle. I would tilt my head upward to absorb its warmth. I would squint my eyes to gaze at the golden ball of fire peeking over the mountaintops and casting light on dark times."

She nodded. "It's beautiful."

He bent and kissed her gently on her bare shoulder. "I'm sorry about yesterday. I should have declined the invitation."

"No. Your aunt had it planned for months before I ever met you. I'm glad we went. I think you needed to clear your mind of Bella. Declaring that you loved me was a little drastic, but I rather liked it. I know it will take time for you to truly feel that way."

"You're wrong, Sophie. I meant it. But simply saying those three words – I love you – doesn't quite convey how I feel. That's what I was doing just now, thinking about you and what to say to you in order to make you believe me."

She rubbed her cheek against his chest. "It doesn't matter, James. I'm happy. Truly, I am." Content as a kitten lapping up cream, she closed her eyes and listened to the strong, steady beat of his heart.

They stood together in silence for a long moment until James began to speak, his voice husky and laden with emotion. "I hope I've found the right words now."

Sophie held her breath as she turned to him, for she didn't know what to expect, only that it would be something special and more wonderful than anything she'd ever imagined possible.

He rubbed his hands along her cool skin when she shivered against the cold air wafting in from the window, and then he gently ran his fingers through her unbound hair. "Your hair is like silk, quite befitting a goddess of the dawn."

She laughed. "You're mistaken, my lord. I'm no goddess, merely a purveyor of poultices."

"You're a healer of damaged hearts." He cast her a breathtaking smile. "I knew you were special the moment I set eyes on you, but didn't dare believe it. We're married less than a week. Your new gowns aren't even ready yet." He kissed her where they stood, bathed in sunlight. "But I've fallen in love with you. Not just in love. In everything with you. I'm in happiness. I'm in hopefulness. I'm in lust with you. Most of all, I awoke beside you and felt in peace for the first time in years."

"Oh, James." Her voice trembled as she spoke. "That's a lovely thing to say."

"It still isn't enough. You're all that's important to me. You're my sunrise, Sophie. You're my morning light. So that's what I shall call you from now on. Sophie, goddess of the morning light. That's what you are. My Sophie. My salvation."

THE END

ALSO BY MEARA PLATT

FARTHINGALE SERIES
My Fair Lily
The Duke I'm Going To Marry
Rules For Reforming A Rake
A Midsummer's Kiss
The Viscount's Rose
Capturing The Heart Of A Cameron

KINDLE WORLD SERIES
Nobody's Angel
Kiss An Angel
Bhrodi's Angel

DARK GARDENS SERIES
Garden of Shadows
Garden of Light
Garden of Dragons
Garden of Destiny

THE BRAYDENS
A Match Made In Duty
Earl of Westcliff

About the Author

Meara Platt is a USA Today bestselling author and an award winning, Amazon UK All-star. She is happily married and has two terrific children. Her favorite place in all the world is England's Lake District, which may not come as a surprise since many of her stories are set in that idyllic landscape, including her Romance Writers of America Golden Heart award winning story released as Book 3 in her paranormal romance Dark Gardens series. Book 1, Garden of Shadows, debuted in December 2016. If you'd like to learn more about the ancient Fae prophecy that is about to unfold in the Dark Gardens series, as well as Meara's lighthearted, international bestselling Regency romances in the Farthingale Series, please visit Meara's website at www.mearaplatt.com.

Made in the USA
Columbia, SC
01 May 2025